DISCOVERING SYNERGY

BY

ELIZABETH KNIGHT

Knight, Elizabeth

Discovering Synergy

Editing: Serious Moonlight Editing & Leavens Editing

Cover artist: RYN KATRYN BOOK COVERS

ISBN: 979-8-88958-009-6 (ebook) / 979-8-88958-009-6 (paperback)

Katie, without you, I wouldn't have written this book twice...

You're right, it was better the second time.

Contents

One

Lailah

No matter how old you are, going to a new school always sucks. When that new school is in an entirely new country? Well, that makes it even worse. After graduation, I didn't know what I wanted to do with my life, so I decided not to force myself into choosing right away. I knew that having no friends and no aspirations would eventually be a problem, especially since I was the only one in my family who had no goals.

After graduation, I helped out at my parents' diner for a few months, which they begrudgingly let me do while I added my name to every college list I could find. None of the schools I applied to seemed quite right though, until I received an email from a school overseas, Ryevick University.

The school's aesthetic enraptured me. Ryevick was somehow both whimsical and modern. The grounds were filled with ornate gardens and buildings with architecture I'd only seen in history books. I've always had a soft spot for history. It's a chance to see what we've lost, but also to see how far we've come. Once I discovered Ryevick required an ancestry test with their application, I sent off my essay and pinprick test the very next day. Three weeks later, I received my acceptance letter in the mail with a full-ride scholarship, housing included.

Ryevick University is located in Drittilyn, a small country in northwest Europe. Although it was a country that I'd never heard of, it seemed too good to be true. Drittilyn is surrounded by so many countries, it's a wonder the common language of the people is English. They drive on the right side of the road, and the US dollar is worth double the value. Who knew that such a magical place existed? And I would never have known about the school in the first place if I hadn't received that email.

I walked out of the airport into a new world, and it was nerve-racking. I couldn't even figure out where the taxis were located. My sense of direction has always been horrible. For the love of God, don't tell me to go north, then head east. Give me landmarks! The last time I thought I could find my way with compass directions, I ended up in the boys' locker room after a football game. So many naked men, my eyes burned for weeks. Not to mention the onslaught of voyeurism jokes from the football players in the halls for the next month.

Following the signs in the airport, I successfully managed to find the area where Taxis were waiting. Walking up to the first one available I smiled at the driver as he helped me with my two suitcases.

"Where to?" the driver asked with a hint of an accent I couldn't place.

"Ryevick University. I'm a new student there," I answered as I slipped into the back of the cab.

"I've done that trip twice today already, so you're in good hands. It'll take us about an hour if the traffic isn't too bad," he said as he pulled away from the curb. "Ever been to Drittilyn before?" he asked.

"No, I've never left the US before," I answered, letting the conversation end as I took in my surroundings.

Once we were outside the city, I felt like we had driven straight into a Jane Austen novel. The rolling hills stretched on for miles. They were dotted with local farms and pastures full of sheep, cows, and goats eating their fill of grass. Amidst the greenery, old brick houses were covered in overgrown ivy. It reminded me of a Thomas Kinkade painting my mother had gotten for Christmas one year. It felt like I was traveling into a dream world, only I could never have come up with something so perfect on my own.

As we got closer to the school, the scenery started to transform into a modern traditional hybrid. New contemporary homes and businesses were mixed in alongside original homesteads. All the while, still retaining the true nature of the surrounding land. The campus covered a vast acreage with historic-looking buildings blending with newer additions, like the dorm that I would be staying in, Ashfall Hall. Thankfully, the taxi driver was familiar with the school grounds, so I didn't have to navigate for him. With my lack of directional skills, we would have been driving around until dark and *still* looking for the dorm.

As I got out of the taxi, I stared up at the two tall, glass buildings that made up the dorms. The tempered glass reflected the waning sunlight, making it seem like it was glowing from the inside out. From the information booklet I had received with my acceptance letter, I knew one building was for the boys, and the other was for the girls. Bridging the two buildings were three common rooms: one on the third floor, one on the fifth floor, and one on the tenth floor. Seeing it in person, I realized the pictures sure as hell didn't do it any justice.

As I looked around, what terrified me the most was ten floors full of complete strangers that I was going to be living with. I'd never had trouble getting along with people, and I was always able to fit in, but my problem was finding a way to stand out, to be noticed, to be remembered. Pushing past my trepidation, I took a deep breath, gripped my suitcases tighter, and strode in through the front doors. No turning back now.

My first impression of the dorm was chaos. In a small sitting area, crying mothers hugged their children goodbye while fathers carried in the last of the belongings. Old friends reunited and shrieked with excitement for the new school year to begin. I was a lost entity in the storm of activity and had no clue what I was supposed to do next.

"Hey, you! Are you here to check in for Ashfall Hall?" a girl carrying a clipboard and a haggard expression on her face asked.

"Yes, I'm Lailah, Lailah Mackenzie," I answered.

The girl scanned down her list of names until she found mine. She frowned and looked up at me. "Oh, you're the scholarship kid."

"Um, I guess," I said, with a shrug.

"Cami!" the girl yelled, startling me. "Your charity case is here for you!"

After the unflattering summons, a small ball of energy popped out of the crowd and walked toward us. Her silver hair was shaved on both sides and the longer strands on top were tousled in every direction. Cami wore a baggy gray sweatshirt that hung off one of her shoulders, proudly displaying her neon-yellow bra strap and tattooed shoulder. I didn't think she was even wearing pants, then she shifted, and saw a sliver of neon-yellow shorts peeking out from underneath her sweatshirt. With wide green eyes and an expressive face, I watched every move she made.

"Welcome to Ashfall Hall. Lailah Mackenzie, I presume," she said, stopping in front of me and thrusting out her hand.

"Ah, yes that's me," I said, shaking her hand.

"I'm Cami, your personal attaché for your first week of school," she said with a wide grin.

"Attaché? Why would I need one of those?" I asked.

"Who knows, but it sounded like fun." Cami shrugged her shoulders and grabbed my suitcase. "Come on, let me show you where you'll be staying."

I followed behind her and asked, "Why was that girl acting all weird about me having a scholarship? Doesn't stuff like that happen all the time?"

"You, missy, are the first female student to ever get a full-ride scholarship. At Ryevick there seems to be a predominantly-male student body," she replied, faking a gag. "So, when a girl gets to come here on a scholarship, you better believe she'll be the talk of the town. They're just jealous because they got way lower scores then you did. So they have to pay. They also miss out on my stellar company, which I find is the bigger loss," Cami said, wagging her eyebrows at me.

I was shocked by this information. Sure, I'd always done well in school, but I wasn't some wonder child. What score could I have possibly gotten on the ACT that would have given me a full-ride scholarship?

"You must be tired from your flight," Cami said offhandedly.

"How did you know I flew here?" I asked in surprise.

Cami winked at me. "With an accent like yours, and the out of control mane you've got going on, it lets me know it's been a long flight. So, my money's on somewhere in the States."

A laugh burst out of me at her bluntness. "I'm from Wisconsin. I come from a small town no one's heard of. The population is a thousand people, most of them farmers."

"Yeah, your clothes look like they come from a place no one's ever heard of either. No need to fret, I've got you covered, sister. I know all the best spots near the school to shop," Cami said, nudging my arm.

Cami and I stepped inside an elevator at the end of the hall, and she hit the button for the tenth floor. It only took a few seconds, and the doors to the elevator opened. Across the entry, floor-to-ceiling windows made up an entire wall, overlooking the campus. Since this was the top floor, I was overlooking the entire campus in all its glory. I saw small groups of people on tours and a large garden across the road that spanned a few acres from what I could see. Close by, there was a large reflecting pool with a stunning fountain in the middle of it. Past that, was a flower garden blooming with color. I spied the top of a huge mansion in the distance, hidden behind ornate windbreak trees. From what I could tell, whoever lived there would give Bill Gates a run for his money.

"Oh my gosh, look at that place. Who lives there?" I gasped.

"Oh, that place. The students call it *The Manor*. The five prodigal sons live there. Trust me, you don't want to mess with them. A cute girl like you would be too tempting for them," Cami said, winking at me. "If I thought I had a shot with you, I'd be first in line, but something tells me that you live on the straight and narrow path."

I blushed under the compliment and her teasing, unsure of what to say. It had been a long time since I'd had a girlfriend to hang out with. I never seemed to find the right group of friends to fit in with. My biggest hope for this new adventure was to be more confident and make some friends. Cami seemed like the perfect person to start with.

"To be honest, I never thought I'd get into this school. It was just so breathtaking online I couldn't help but send in my application. Then, to find out I not only got in but got a full ride... I couldn't believe it," I said, following Cami as she walked down the hall.

"I guess it's a pretty cool place. This building is super strange though, because none of the dorm rooms have windows. Weird, right? They say this building was funded by a major corporation that wanted to construct an *energy-efficient* building," Cami said, using air quotations. "Not sure how trapping us in a box without sunlight is energy efficient, but whatever. The payoff is when you walk out of your room, you'll have one of the best views of the grounds. Plus, you'll be close to the common room and the elevator," she continued as she walked.

"I never knew a place like this could exist," I muttered to myself. "The dorms seem so modern whereas the school seems to be stuck in a time capsule."

"This is you," Cami said excitedly, guiding me to the door and waving a keycard in front of the sensor.

I expected the room to be tiny with two twin beds, two desks, and a small closet, but that's not what I found when I opened the door. This quaint room clearly was meant for one person. The main area was open and simple. A brown loveseat and a low table made up the living room area. To the left of the couch was a bare bed, waiting for me to dress it. Along another wall, there was a desk with a chair that would be perfect for doing schoolwork. On the opposite side of the room was a wall covered in wooden cubby squares for storage.

"So, what do you think?" Cami asked with a grin and her hands on her hips.

"I can't believe this is really going to be my dorm room for the next year," I said, returning her smile. "This will be the first time I'll be on my own."

"Now it's time to party like a rock star! I saw that you shipped some boxes. I might know a guy who can help bring those up if you want me to ask," Cami offered. "Oh, before I forget, classes start on Monday, so make sure you have everything you need by Sunday. Normally, all the shops close early on Saturdays and Sundays, but lucky for you, they're open late this weekend."

"Thank you for everything," I said, feeling my eyelids drooping as a wave of tiredness hit me. "I don't know what I would've done trying to manage this on my own."

"Girl, don't stress it. Hey, if you want, I can go with you into town and help you find things you need," Cami offered, squeezing my arm reassuringly.

I nodded. "Oh, God, I would love you forever; you have no idea how bad I am with directions. I might get lost and never be heard from again if I tried to go alone."

Cami laughed like I made a joke. Little did she know how bad it really was. "Let me see if I can get those boxes up here so you can take a nap, you're fading faster than a stoner."

As Cami left my room, I tried to stay awake by unpacking my suitcase. I found a dresser built into the wall by the cubbies, and I thought that was a brilliant idea since space was limited. When I finally finished putting away the basics of my life, I trudged down the hall to find the bathroom. I badly needed to wash up, fifteen hours on a plane was brutal, and I felt gross.

I found the girls' bathroom in the opposite direction of the common room, as far away from my room as possible. I walked in carrying my gallon Ziplock bag of toiletries and set it on the long counter of sinks. I looked up at the mirror and groaned, my mascara had given me a lovely raccoon shadow to compliment my crystal-blue eyes. I blew a rogue strand of my curly blonde hair out of my face as I bent down to wash my face. It wasn't until I had rinsed off that I'd forgotten that I needed a towel. I looked around for something to use and found the dispenser for paper towels. I grabbed a few and started to dab at my face.

"Looks like the charity case can't even afford a towel," a girl commented as she passed me, coming out of one of the showers.

"I have one," I called after her as she left. "I just forgot it in my room."

Just what I needed: catty girls to deal with. I hope this whole scholarship thing will blow over fast.

Not feeling very optimistic, I grabbed my Ziplock and left the bathroom without doing anything to the mass of curls on my head. Besides, I didn't want to be gone too long in case Cami's connection brought up my stuff. Sure enough, when I got back, two boxes were sitting outside my door. The third and last box was filled with books, and I kind of felt bad for whoever was roped into bringing it up. When I packed, there was no way I could leave behind the closest things to friends that I had. Shoving the first boxes in my room, I started to remove the tape when a knock sounded at my door.

"I have the last of your things. If you don't mind opening the door, this one is a bit heavy," a deep voice came from the other side.

"Be there in a sec," I answered, trotting over to the door.

I opened it to find a large black man with a charming smile on his face. I pulled the door open the rest of the way so he could walk in. As he set the box down, I noticed the back of his black polo read *Security*.

I didn't realize Cami would send someone from security to carry my boxes.

"Thank you very much for bringing all this up. I hope it wasn't too much trouble. I wasn't sure how much I was going to need from home," I said, a little embarrassed by the amount that I'd packed. It was almost as if I'd moved half my room by the time I'd packed everything.

"No trouble at all, Cami's a good egg with all her crazy," he said with a conspiratorial grin that I couldn't help but reciprocate.

"I'm sorry, I feel so rude; I didn't even ask your name. I'm Lailah," I said, holding out my hand.

"Tony," he said, swallowing my own hand with his.

"Nice to meet you, Tony. How did Cami manage to rope you into helping me out? I'm sure working security has you very busy today with all the students and families coming and going," I mused.

Tony just shrugged his broad shoulders. "This building is part of my zone, so when she asked me to help a damsel in distress—her words, mind you—I couldn't refuse. She doesn't ask for too many favors, and she doesn't exactly blend in at this school, so making real friends is a little tough."

"Seriously? I would have guessed Cami is the person everyone would want to be friends with," I said in shock.

"I agree, but when your family has ties to the five most eligible men on campus, you never know who's truly your friend," Tony explained.

I nodded my head and tried to muse that over. I'd never had any connections with desirable people, so I had no way to relate. "Don't worry, I have no interest in getting involved in the school drama. I just want to enjoy my first year of college and being out on my own."

"Let's make a deal. You keep an eye on her for me, and if you ever find yourself in trouble, I'd be happy to come to help you out," Tony said and pulled out a card from his back pocket. "Here's my cell number; call or text me anytime if you need me."

"Thanks," I said, taking the card and feeling more at ease, now that I had someone looking out for me.

After Tony left, I looked at the unopened boxes on the floor. "Well, if I'm going to sleep tonight, I might need to unbox these. I wouldn't want people thinking I can't afford sheets," I said, opening the box I knew had my sheets and towels in them.

Once the bed was made, I gave in to my exhaustion and curled up, falling asleep the moment my head hit the pillow.

Two

Lailah

Having slept peacefully through the night, I woke up feeling refreshed and excited. I glanced over at the clock and saw it was well into the day. *How had I slept till almost noon?* I wandered over to the dresser and grabbed fresh clothes for the day. I pulled on some yoga pants and an oversized Notre Dame hoodie that my brother Dylan had given me. That he had given me in hopes that I'd follow in his footsteps.

I decided to finish unpacking and opened the box that had 'books' written on it. I peeled off the tape and started placing the books in the cubbies along the wall. Seeing all my favorite books made me feel more at home. Just when I was going to open the next box, someone knocked on the door. Curious to see who it could be, I opened the door and smiled.

"Did Tony bring up your stuff last night?" Cami asked, brushing past me and jumping on my rumpled bed.

"Yeah, thanks for asking him. He's super nice," I said, walking back over to my boxes.

"Tony has been with Ryevick for ages. He knows my sisters, so when I started here last year, they had him keep an eye on me to make sure I didn't do anything too crazy," she said, flopping onto her belly to watch me unpack while kicking her feet.

I opened the next box and Elle the elephant, my favorite stuffed animal, popped out and landed on the floor. Cami jumped off the bed and picked Elle up before I could even blink.

"This is so cute!" Cami squealed.

I laughed at her excitement. I'd wanted to take Elle on the plane with me, but I didn't think I could handle the looks I would have gotten from people. Now that I'd seen how being the scholarship student had drawn so much attention, I was glad I hadn't added to it.

Carefully, I pulled out the family photo my mom had packed for me. After my graduation, she'd made us all get dressed up and take a *fancy* family photo. I went to go set it on the desk, but Cami was right at my elbow, pulling the frame out of my hands.

"Is this your family?"

"Yup, those are my parents, Bonnie and Luke. They own the best diner in my hometown, called Percy's. The good-looking guy is my older brother Dylan. He just graduated from Notre Dame this past summer with his MBA and is going back to get a law degree. He has always wanted to take over our parents' diner when they retire, so he decided to stay in school a little longer. The little punk next to me, who looks like he has been tortured for the past hour, is Kyle. He's a freshman in high school this year." As I talked about them, I felt tears well up in my eyes.

I'd been *so* good about not crying through this whole thing. Mom had bawled her eyes out as I got on the plane, but I'd managed to hold it together. Apparently, this was the moment it all started to hit me like a ton of bricks. I was in a completely different country, with an ocean and a fifteen-hour flight between us. I wasn't going to be able to just drive a few hours and be home for a weekend like Dylan could.

"Oh, hun, don't cry," Cami said as she threw her arms around me. "I'm sorry. I didn't mean to make you sad. Let's go out this afternoon, and I'll show you around town. That will cheer you up."

As much as I appreciated her comfort, I couldn't help but giggle because she was so short, her head was resting perfectly on my boobs. That thought lightened my mood, and I brushed away the tears.

"That sounds like fun," I said, patting her on the back before I pulled out of her hug. "So, tell me about you."

Cami walked back to my bed and fell backward on it again. "Me? Well, my room is one floor down, right next to the elevator, lucky number six. Thank God I don't have a roommate this year. The girl I lived last year with was the worst. Hmm, let's see, what else," Cami said, sitting up suddenly. "Oh! I'm going to school for journalism! I love to get all up in people's business, so my parents suggested that I make it a job."

I shook my head and laughed as I continued to pull stuff out of the boxes and put it away. "You mentioned Tony knew your sisters, are they older or younger?"

"I have two older sisters, but one's a half-sister. They're cool, I guess. They are always trying to push me into being more involved in the family business," Cami said, scrunching up her face in distaste.

"That's funny, my parents couldn't wait to get me *out* of the family business. Since Dylan was already planning on taking it over, they didn't see the need for me to waste my potential. I think they have me mixed up with Kyle, because he's the wonder child. He's at this crazy prep school an hour away from home that my mom has to drive him to every day," I explained. "When I said that I didn't understand how I got a scholarship for this school, I wasn't kidding. I'm a good student, but nothing that could match up to his abilities."

"They must have seen something impressive about you if they gave you one of the four scholarships they have for the year," Cami countered.

"The only thing I'm really good at is running track and hurdles, but this school doesn't have anything sports-related on campus," I said, sitting on the couch.

"Oh, girl, you will never catch me running. I would much rather take out what's chasing me than run from it," Cami said, standing up. She waved at me to follow her. "Come on, let's go get some lunch. There's a great little sandwich place in Nettleton. And don't forget to bring your class list so we can grab your books."

"I really need a shower. Can we go after I get ready quick?" I asked Cami before she could drag me out the door.

She gave me a once-over and nodded. "That might be a good idea." She walked over to my dresser and started rifling through my clothes. When she got to my T-shirt drawer, she started laughing. "These are gold, girl. I couldn't have picked better. Where did you get them?"

"My brothers started my collection of sassy shirts after they broke into my room and read my journal from when I was in middle school. They said my inner snark needed an outlet, so for every birthday and Christmas, I get new shirts that they find. After a while, I embraced it and started buying some of my own," I said, smiling and remembering how it all started.

"Sounds like your brothers and I would get along," Cami said, handing me a stack of clothes. "Now, go shower! We have important shenanigans to get up to!"

I showered as fast as I could so she wouldn't have to wait too long. I tore a comb through my curly hair as it fell to the middle of my back. There was no time to dry it with my diffuser, so I threw some curl cream in and called it good. I wiggled into the jeans Cami had grabbed and looked at what shirt she picked out. It said, "I'm not short, I'm concentrated awesome." I laughed and put it on. I'd never thought of myself as tall, but compared to Cami, I was. Ready for the day, I headed back to my room to grab the rest of my stuff so we could head out.

"So, how are we getting to town? Do they have a shuttle for the students to use?" I asked, slipping on some sandals.

Cami looked at me like I had just asked her if she wanted to eat dirt. "Oh, my poor, sweet country bumpkin, that will never happen. I have a car here. I'll drive—unless you know how to drive a stick?"

I shook my head vigorously. "Trust me, you do not want me driving; we'll end up in another country."

"Perfect! I love driving!" Cami said, grabbing a purse that she must've brought up while I was in the shower.

I walked with Cami to the elevator, and we exited the dorm out the back, where the student parking was. I scanned the cars, wondering which one was hers. All of them looked sleek and expensive. I would only ever own one in my dreams. Cami walked up to a small neon-green car with black detailing on it. The car chirped as she unlocked it, and she waved for me to hurry up. The car didn't look like it could hold more than two people, but once I was inside, I was surprised by how roomy it was.

"What kind of car is this?" I asked.

Before she answered, she hit a button, and the fabric roof started to roll back, letting in the sunlight and fresh air. "It's a Fiat 500, custom color, of course. I can't get lost in the parking lot looking for this little guy."

I laughed, thinking that is exactly something I would need to do when I got my next car. My laughing got cut short as Cami dropped the clutch, and we rocketed out of the parking spot and onto the street. Looked like I was going to die before I even got to start school.

"Cami! Slow the hell down!" I yelled after clutching the armrests.

"Calm your tits, we'll be just fine. I drive like this all the time. Why do you think I bought this car?" Cami said and giggled as she turned on the radio, blasting the car with the top ten hits.

My wild curls whipped around my head, slapping me in the face as we went. Thankfully, I always kept a scrunchie on my wrist for moments like this. I trapped my hair in a messy bun on my head, and I was now able to at least see some of the blurring scenery as we went. Unsurprisingly, it didn't take us long to get into town and for Cami to swoop into a parking spot. As she cut the engine, she looked over at me triumphantly, like keeping us alive was noteworthy.

It took me a minute to get out of the car and get my equilibrium back. Once I got past the dizziness, I finally had a chance to look around. The little town of Nettleton had been well-preserved. All the modern cars that were parked along the stone-faced shops looked so out of place. The tires of the cars passing by sounded funny as they rolled over the cobblestone roadway. Each shop had a hand-painted, wooden sign that let shoppers know what they offered inside. Groups of students, full of energy, laughed and dashed in and out of the stores with loaded bags.

"Come on, the sandwich shop is just around the corner," Cami said, locking the car and walking away.

Slipping my purse over my shoulder, I jogged after her. For a person with such short legs, she moved superfast. I couldn't get over the feeling that I was on a movie set or something. There's no way a place like this could be around in real life. Maybe it was just because I hadn't traveled out of my home state, but this felt strange.

The sandwich shop was cute. We ordered our sandwiches at the counter and then found a place to sit and eat. We decided to eat inside since the last of the summer heat was still hanging on.

"Besides your school supplies, is there anything else we need to get you while you're in town?" Cami asked as we cleaned up after our meal.

"Not that I can think of, but I'm sure I've missed something. Guess we'll just have to make another trip," I said, smiling because I liked the idea of having a friend to go shopping with.

"To make the most of today, I figured we need to stop in every shop, so you at least know what is available. For research, of course," Cami said, winking at me.

Cami was going to be good at helping me get out of my own bubble. "Where to first?" I asked.

"Seeing as we just finished lunch, I think dessert is in order. There is a kick-ass bakery just up the way that you have to try," Cami said, holding the door open for us to leave.

Cami wasn't lying when she said the bakery was awesome. Everything they displayed looked so decadent. As I scanned the case, I stumbled upon the cookie section and was immediately drawn to the colorful ones. Sugar cookies were my favorite thing in the world. My mother made the best soft-textured sugar cookies ever. She promised to send me a care package of them at some point, but I knew I would have to find a new dealer for my obsession.

"Would you like a sample?" the older woman behind the counter asked.

"Yes, I would love to try them," I said, practically bouncing with joy.

"Did you want to try the frosted or soft kind?" she asked.

"Um, the soft, please," I said, lifting my hands to take the chunk of cookie she'd cut for me.

I popped the morsel into my mouth and hummed with delight. It was almost as perfect as my mother's recipe, and that was singing some high praise. "I would like to buy two of them, please."

The woman wrapped up the two cookies for me and handed them to me when I'd paid.

"You seemed pretty happy to get those cookies," Cami commented, giggling.

"They say that diamonds are the way to a woman's heart, but for me, it's through sugar cookies." I laughed and pulled out a cookie.

As we exited the bakery, I lifted the cookie to my mouth, when I bumped into someone and dropped the cookie. I stared in shock at the crushed bit of cookie on the sidewalk and looked up to glare at whoever ran into me. Cami beat me to it.

"God! Parker! You're such an idiot! Don't you know to look where you're going? You totally smashed her cookie, asshole," Cami snapped at the guy who'd run into me.

"Fuck off, Cami, it was an accident," Parker said, going toe to toe with Cami.

Parker was handsome, like came-down-from-Mount-Olympus handsome. He was tall and buff like a football player, but I could tell he would still move with agile grace. His spiky red hair, warm brown eyes, and full lips perfectly complemented his strong facial features. He also seemed to have quite the female posse shadowing him. There were five girls behind him frowning at us.

"At least buy the girl another cookie to make up for your complete incompetence," Cami said with her hands on her hips, eliciting gasps from the other girls.

Parker looked up at me as if he was noticing me for the first time. "I'm sorry I killed your cookie. I wasn't expecting an angel to come crashing into town, let alone crash into one myself. If I'd known, I would have been paying better attention."

I almost choked on my own spit hearing this guy making a pass at me. I had only ever had one boyfriend before, and that hadn't ended very well. I cleared my throat quietly, trying to pull my act together.

"It happens. But make sure you're watching out for people next time," I said, trying to sound as disapproving as I felt, though I was flustered by his attention.

"Let me make up for it by getting you another cookie. It's the least I can do," he said, ducking into the shop without waiting for an answer and ignoring the fact that Cami came up with the idea first.

Cami and I waited awkwardly outside with the other girls he had been hanging out with. I couldn't help but fidget uncomfortably. Thankfully, Parker didn't take long, and he reappeared with a fresh sugar cookie for me.

He handed it over with a flourishing bow. "Might I know the name of the fair maiden this cookie is for?"

"Lailah, that's my name," I said lamely. Avoiding his eyes as I added the cookie to the bag with the other one I bought for safekeeping, not wanting to risk it while he was still around.

God! Why am I so awkward when it comes to good-looking guys?

"Lailah. A lovely name for a lovely lady. Where are you guys off to next? I would like to offer my escort services to make sure this cookie remains unharmed," Parker said, grinning again.

"We don't need your help! It looks like you have enough women you're dealing with today. No need to worry about us. I've got this covered," Cami said, grabbing my arm and pulling me away without a second thought. "We need to hit up the bookstore before we have that leech trying to attach himself to us for the rest of the day."

"What's his deal?" I asked, surprised at how much he'd gotten under Cami's skin.

"He's one of the five that live in The Manor," Cami said as we crossed the street and headed for a building that had a line wrapped around the corner.

"Cami! Lailah! Wait up!" Parker yelled from behind us.

I looked over my shoulder to see him running after us, free of his fan club. Cami didn't slow at all but sped up instead. Parker jogged up to us and then fell into step on my other side.

"Did you guys hear me?" he asked.

"We heard, just didn't care," Cami retorted.

"Geeze, Cami! Why do you have to be such a hard-ass all the time?" Parker grumbled.

Cami stopped and looked at him with a frown. "Parker, we've known each other for almost our entire lives, I know Lailah is not going to be your next plaything. I am doing you both a favor, just trust me on this."

I felt like there was more to that statement than I got at face value, but it didn't seem to matter to Parker.

"Whatever; I can be friends with Lailah," he said and turned to me. "Would you like to be my friend?"

My head was spinning from all their back and forth. "All I want to do is go to school and keep out of the drama. I just want a normal college experience."

"I didn't hear a no in there," Parker said, smiling and walking with us toward the bookstore.

As we approached, I noticed a familiar security guard at the front of the line. "Wow! They need a bookstore bouncer?" I asked.

"Yup, that's Tony. He is a nice guy; he also works for the school security team," Parker said as he walked up to Tony.

"Hey, Lailah, good to see you again," Tony said, winking. "I see you're already making more friends. You let me know if Parker here ever gets out of hand, I'll straighten him out for ya."

"Not cool, man. Don't be spreading lies about me," Parker said, punching Tony's arm.

Ignoring Parker, Tony turned to me. "You got your list of books?"

"Yeah, I have it right here," I said, showing it to him.

"Well, in you go then," he said, holding the door open for us and grinning. "Not you, Parker, I know you don't need anything from the bookstore," Tony said, grabbing Parker's shoulder.

Cami proceeded to stick her tongue out at him as she passed him into the bookstore. "Thanks a million, Tony! You're a real gem, and don't let anyone tell you any different."

Three

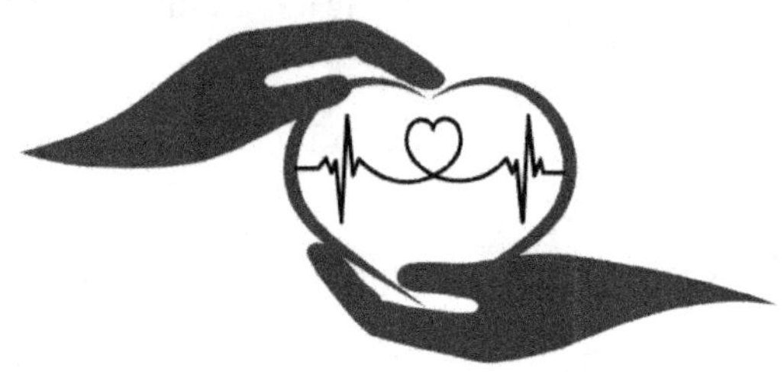

Parker

I watched the girls enter the bookstore and then turned to Tony. "What gives, man? Why is Cami back at school anyway?"

"You know I can't tell you stuff like that, no matter who you are. If you want to know, ask Beth," Tony said, crossing his arms.

"Have any of the other guys seen her back at school?" I pressed.

"Talk to Beth," Tony said, unwilling to budge.

"What happened to pals before gals? Man code? Is nothing sacred?" I asked, shaking my head slowly.

"Leave, Parker. You can't wait out here until they come back out," Tony said, catching on to my plan.

"Fine. I'm going. But know that I'm disappointed in you, Tony," I said over my shoulder.

After I walked down the block, I found a bench to sit on. I pulled out my phone and sent Beth a text.

> Me: **Hey, I ran into Cami... didn't know she was coming back.**

I set my phone down and gave her a few minutes to answer. My thoughts drifted to the girl Cami was with—Lailah. I felt awful that I ran into her and killed her cookie. I hated that it happened to such an attractive girl, too. I'm sure Cami is filling her head full of lies about me just for her own enjoyment.

Lailah was not like the typical girls who came to our school. She didn't seem rich, power-hungry, or a gold digger. No, I got a small-town vibe from her. She didn't need makeup to look beautiful or have perfectly-styled hair. I liked that she was comfortable in her own skin. It was super attractive in a whole new way. I would even say there was something between us. It was like my powers recognized that she was unique as well. *Hmm, I wonder if Beth knows anything about her?*

My phone buzzed with Beth's response.

> Beth: **Leave her alone, Parker. It took a lot of convincing to get her to come back. I don't need you sticking your nose in this.**

> Me: **That's harsh, Miss B. Hey! Do you know anything about her friend Lailah?**

Beth: **She's a scholarship student, freshman, why do you ask?**

Me: **dk. I just felt something when I ran into her and wondered if you had any intel on her**

Beth: **Parker, I am not your dating service, if you want to know something, maybe you should talk to her. Oh, and don't call me Miss B.**

I shook my head, knowing that was all I was going to get out of her. She was right about one thing; I was definitely going to need to talk to Lailah again.

Four

Lailah

For the rest of the weekend, Cami and I hung out, and she showed me the basics of dorm life. She also helped me find the dining hall after I failed to find it on my own and spent a good hour wandering around. Having Cami around also seemed to keep people from making snide remarks about my scholarship. I hoped that the novelty of it would fade soon.

"I know you don't have classes tomorrow because it's orientation day, but I could really use your help finding the auditorium," I begged Cami as we headed back to the dorm after dinner.

"You're lucky I like you, Lala," Cami said, using the nickname she had picked for me. "What time do you need to be there?"

"You're a lifesaver, Cami," I said, and I hugged her. "It starts at eight."

"Why are you taking that stupid class anyway? Who actually signs up for *Freshman* 101?" Cami grumbled.

"It's University 101 Cami, and I've been so fascinated with the school, I thought taking a class about it would be fun," I said, defending my choice.

"Whatever. I'll make sure I get you to your lame class tomorrow, but you're buying my coffee," she said, waving goodnight to me as she got off the elevator on her floor.

The next day I would be starting my first day as a college student, it was exciting and terrifying at the same time. Thankfully, I had managed to figure out a plan with Cami so she could help me get to classes for the first week. We had a lot of classes in the same buildings, or at least they were on the way, so it worked out easily enough. When I reached my room, I sorted through what books I would need and double-checked the syllabus to make sure I didn't forget anything. Feeling as ready as I was going to be, I set my alarm for six-thirty and curled up in bed with my favorite book. I needed to end the night with a little Mr. Darcy.

"Rise and shine! This is your six-thirty-a.m. alarm! The forecast today is overcast with a high of sixty-eight degrees!"

I rolled over and groped around for my phone on the nightstand to turn off my alarm. I groaned as I rubbed the sleep out of my eyes and remembered that I hadn't given myself a huge amount of time to get ready. I shuffled my way down the hall to the bathroom. After washing my face and brushing my teeth, I tackled my hair. I left it down and contemplated how it looked. I felt like the cowardly lion from the *Wizard of Oz* with my wild curls loose. I tried to pin it up in a cute way but failed to find something that worked. Giving up, I just piled it on top of my head again in my usual messy bun. I brushed on some mascara and filled in my brows, trying to make it look like I made an extra effort.

Back in my room, I pulled out my nice white skinny jeans and a silky blush-colored top to go with it. After slipping my shoes on, I was about to leave to meet Cami in the lobby when I paused to grab my long olive sweater just in case the classroom got cold. I threw my messenger bag across my body, and I did one last sweep of the room to make sure I didn't forget anything. Satisfied, I headed down to meet Cami so we could grab a coffee on the way to my class.

It wasn't hard to spot Cami, half asleep in one of the lobby armchairs. "Lala, I'm not sure this friendship is going to work out if you're going to make me do this all the time."

I walked over and pulled her out of the chair. "Come on. I'll get you the biggest cup of coffee the school has to offer."

Cami grunted at this and followed me out the door. Once we crossed the street onto the main campus, Cami took over leading the way. We reached the coffee shop, and thankfully, it wasn't packed.

"Morning, Cami! Want your usual extra-large black coffee?" the guy taking orders asked.

I raised my eyebrows at Cami, surprised to see this guy knew her and her order so readily. Cami just shrugged at me. "I like coffee, so sue me."

"I'm paying for her addiction today. Could you add a chai tea latte for me?"

Cami gave me a funny look as the barista handed over her massive cup of coffee. "You make fun of me for my coffee, and yet you order that crap?"

"I love the smell of coffee but never acquired a taste for it," I said, walking over to the pickup counter.

"Just so we're clear, I am never ordering that for you. I will not have anyone thinking that I'm drinking that froufrou shit,"

Cami said, walking out of the coffee shop. I grabbed my drink and hurried after her.

"I never would have guessed you'd be so *judgmental* over my drink choices," I said, teasing her and knowing that her attitude would lighten up as she drank her coffee.

Cami's only response was a grunt from behind the lid of her coffee cup. I took in the sights of the school as we walked through the main buildings. The architecture was beautiful and showed the beauty of an age gone by. The intricate craftsmanship of each door, window, and archway could never be replicated. Finally reaching the core of the school, I noticed all the other students bustling about and heading to class. They milled about, chatting with friends or looking at school maps trying to find the right building. I was so grateful to have Cami at my side, so I didn't have to wander for hours. Even with a map, I would have been lost in less than ten seconds.

"Remind me again. You have this class, and then when am I supposed to check in with you?" Cami asked as we reached the auditorium doors.

"This class has two parts today. We have the class here for an hour, then we go on a tour of the grounds. They didn't say how long it would take, so I'll just text you when I get done and tell you where I'm at," I said, double-checking that I had my phone on me.

"Works for me. Make good choices and learn lots!" Cami said, waving as she walked away.

I pulled open the old, heavy wooden door and walked in. The auditorium had stadium seating and a stage with a podium in the front. I found a seat in the middle section for the best view and took out a notebook and pen.

A girl behind me snickered to her friend. "Look at the good little scholarship student, she thinks she's going to learn something in this class."

I reached my breaking point with all the snide scholarship remarks. I turned slightly in my seat and looked over my shoulder. "If you think this class is so lame, why did you decide to take it?"

Not feeling the need to wait for an answer, I faced forward again just in time to see the teacher walk up to the podium. He was an older man with white hair that was cut close to his head, trying to diminish the fact that he was balding. His face was full of laugh lines, giving me a clue to his personality. His brown eyes were intelligent and warm as he looked out over the room.

"Welcome, students! I'm Mr. Phillips, your professor for University 101. In this class, we will be learning about the history of our school and the town surrounding it. I hope that by the end of this semester, you will have a greater appreciation for the history that you get to experience every day," Professor Phillips said, greeting the class.

"Today, our class will be broken up into two sections. First, we will go over the syllabus and my expectations for my students. Then, we will head out for a tour of the grounds. We have combined all the different classes together for today, so the Student Council will be helping me out since I am severely outnumbered by all of you," he said with a smile and a wink that made everyone laugh.

I could tell I was going to like learning from Mr. Phillips. I pulled out my syllabus to follow along as he went over it. The class went by quickly, and soon, we were all asked to gather in the quad for the tour. I filed out of the auditorium and pitched my empty cup. I followed the crowd, hoping that they would lead me to where I was supposed to be. Some students broke off to the left, chatting with one another, and the other group went straight. I took a guess and followed the group going straight.

"All the students going on the tour need to split up into their appropriate class groups. I need the eight o'clock class on my left, noon in the middle, and the five o'clock class on the far right," a girl shouted over the group. I assumed that she was part of the Student Council.

I walked over to the left group and waited, looking around at all the people running from building to building. I was so distracted, I didn't notice that my group left for the tour. Not wanting to get left behind, I jumped into the noon-class group before I could get lost. I was totally absorbed in the tour and all the history of each building. Who wouldn't find this stuff interesting?

"Aiden Ryevick founded this school in 1623 at the end of the Renaissance and entering into the Baroque period. At this time, churches were overseeing the type of art being produced, so Aiden Ryevick decided to found his own school specializing in the arts," our student tour guide shared as we passed a statue of the founder. "We have come to find out that he lied to the Catholic church about adhering to the restrictions placed on all creations produced by artists. He was successful at the time because he put in the chapel, which we now use as an auditorium, as a facade."

As the tour went on, I learned more about Ryevick's founder and his drive to free artists and later scientists of all kinds, so they could dive further into their fields. We moved past several other buildings and went out into the gardens.

"Our school prides itself on being fully self-sufficient, so we aren't taking away from the community around us. The school has its own livestock, vegetable gardens, and grain fields that are used to make all the food here on campus. We also have our own herb garden that our medical students use to produce modern and holistic medicine."

I was so distracted by all the indigenous plants that I had to stop to investigate. Unfortunately, when I looked up, I couldn't find my group.

Why do I always do this? I know I get lost all the time, so I should be better at staying with the group.

I remembered them saying that they would be heading to the garden maze next. I looked around, hoping I might see something that would point me in that direction, but with no luck, I headed off to the right, praying that was the direction I needed to go. I wandered for a while and ended up by the reflecting pool I had seen from the dorm windows—nowhere near where I needed to be.

Lost on the school grounds, I sat on the edge of the reflecting pool, letting my face fall into my hands. "Are you okay?" a voice said, making me jump.

I looked up and was shocked to see a gorgeous man peering down at me. He was tall and attractive, just like Parker, that other guy I had met in town. His clothes were of the latest fashion and very high-end but still practical. His rich-brown hair was styled in the latest trend—short on the sides but longer strands swept back on the top. Did this school only have gorgeous model-esque students attending here? His warm hazel eyes were still looking at me, filled with concern, and I realized then that he was still waiting for my answer.

"I am hopelessly lost. I was on a tour of the school, but I got distracted and lost my group," I admitted as my cheeks heated.

"Yeah, this school is huge, it takes some getting used to. Would you like me to help you find your group? I'm actually supposed to be helping out with the tours anyway, but another obligation made me very late," he said and held out a hand to help me up.

I reached out and let him pull me to my feet. When his skin touched mine, a slight tingle ran down my arm, causing me to shiver slightly. I smiled up at him awkwardly, hoping he didn't notice my reaction to his touch. I was acting like I didn't know how to be around attractive guys. I took that moment to collect myself and brush off the back of my pants.

"I'm Brayden, by the way," he said, giving me a small smile.

"I'm Lailah," I said, returning his smile. "Thanks for offering to help me out. Let's just say I'm directionally challenged, and that's a severe understatement. I would have wandered around out here till I gave up and went back to my dorm. I can at least see that clear as day," I said, gesturing to Ashfall behind me.

"Ah, you're staying in Ashfall Hall. I heard that the rooms don't have windows. Is it true?" he asked as we started walking along the edge of the reflecting pool.

"Yup, but with the school load I decided on, I'm not sure I'll be around much except to sleep. Thankfully, there are common rooms that have massive windows to make up for it." I chuckled.

"Well, at Aiden House, there are lots of windows and plenty of sunlight. The concept of not having a window and natural light freaks me out a little. As an agricultural major, you could say I'm pretty attached to the outdoors," Brayden said with a grin.

"Aiden House?" I asked. "I don't think I know that dorm."

"Most of the students here call it The Manor," Brayden clarified for me.

I stopped in my tracks and gaped at him. "You're one of the five?"

Brayden turned to look at me. "Is that a problem?"

"No, I guess not. The campus is so big, I just thought the odds of me running into any of you would be rare, and now I've met two of you," I said. I'm not sure why it surprised me.

"Oh? Who else have you met?" Brayden inquired, starting to walk again.

"My friend Cami and I ran into Parker when we were in town."

"You know Cami? What a small world! Our families have known each other for a long time. We grew up together," Brayden said.

"Funny how that works. I grew up in a small town where everyone knows everyone. Although it sucks when people who used to be your friends aren't anymore. It makes things awkward because they live down the street." I was rambling.

"I'm sure that would be challenging. I'm sorry to hear that happened. Is that why you decided to come all this way to attend college?" Brayden asked.

Why am I telling him all this? I don't even know him. He's just so easy to talk to. Plus, he keeps asking questions, it would be rude of me not to answer—*right?*

"Yes and no. I knew that I wanted a change, but I didn't know what exactly. Then I got an email from Ryevick University after my parents signed me up for this crazy college finder website. Funny, what really got me excited about this place was the history, the different culture, and the art. Like that fountain, for example." I pointed to the huge fountain in the middle of the reflecting pool. I'd seen a picture on the website, but seeing it in person, it was much more impressive.

Brayden looked to where I was pointing and smiled. "That is one of my favorites. Would you like to hear the story behind it? But I have to warn you, it's a bit fanciful."

"Now you're just taunting me," I said, nudging his arm encouragingly.

"The story claims that Aiden Ryevick started going crazy in his old age. This fountain was the last piece he created before he lost his mind and died. When people asked him what it represented, he would explain it like this." He was setting up the tale expertly. "As you can see, there are five human figures holding hands with an additional human figure standing in the middle of them. He said that each one represented an element."

I frowned. "Wait. I thought there were only four elements: earth, wind, water, and fire. What are the other two?"

"The fifth element is less commonly known; it is called by a few different names. Some people call it aether and others call it spirit. I actually have a friend who likes to call it heart." His eyes were shining with mystery. "The final one in the middle is what Aiden called Synergy."

"Synergy isn't an element at all. It's more of an action, isn't it?" I asked, knowing I had heard the word before.

"Synergy means to combine one or more elements to make them stronger," Brayden said, giving me an answer straight from the dictionary.

"Okay, so how do the elements relate to the figures in the fountain?" I asked.

"This is where the fiction comes into play. He explained to one of his students that five men were gifted with these elemental powers by angels. If they fought for good and didn't turn evil, then one day, they would be gifted a great power. This power was titled Synergy. These magical warriors were not told what Synergy would be or when it would appear, they just had to continue defending the world from demons, and they would someday be rewarded. Aiden had always envisioned that Synergy would be another human, so he made this fountain to represent the five warriors and when they were gifted Synergy." He looked at me out of the corner of his eye.

I took in the fountain with a whole new perspective. I noticed that each of the figures had a symbol carved into it. I could only assume the symbols represented each element. "That is a beautiful story; did they ever discover their hidden Synergy?" I asked, looking back at Brayden.

A shadow of sadness flickered through his eyes before he started walking away from the fountain. "The story, as far as I know, hasn't been finished yet; seems they're still in an endless journey of looking and waiting."

"Stories like that are why I fell in love with history. If I'd never come here to try something new, then I would've never known this amazing story about this school. Sure, it might be fiction, but what life doesn't need a little dash of fantasy to make it interesting?"

"I can see why you and Cami are friends; she sees the world through a technicolor lens and hates to be sucked into the humdrum of life," he said with a wistfulness in his voice. "Ah, look. There are our tour groups. Seems we're meeting them on their way over to the reflecting pool."

Brayden and I waited till the groups caught up to us, and I filed into one, not caring if it was the right one. This time I was determined to stick with them and not get left behind again. Before I could wander too far off, Brayden gently grabbed my elbow.

"It was lovely to meet you, Lailah; I hope we run into each other again some time," Brayden said with a smile that gave me butterflies.

"I would like that. Maybe you can share some more stories with me about the school," I said, blushing and falling in with my original class group.

Five

Brayden

I was having a hard time staying focused as I helped with the rest of the tour. Thankfully, I didn't have to do much. I answered any questions that the students had, but even then, I gave half-hearted answers. My mind kept wandering back to those clear blue eyes and long golden hair. I'd originally planned to just walk past her because I was already late for the tour. Yet seeing her lost and alone made my protective instincts run wild. Something about Lailah drew me in. I could've sworn that my powers reacted when I grasped her hand.

I had watched her face carefully as I told the story about the Elementi, and she listened with rapt attention. What would she do if she knew the story was true? Would she still see it as something so magical? What would she do if she knew the current five Elementi Warriors were actually failures?

In the last week, demons had been sneaking onto the school grounds more and more. Every night, the five of us took turns patrolling the school. There seemed to be something drawing them here. The previous generations of Elementi Warriors had always been able to band together as a united front and keep up the wards guarding the school. We had failed to find a way to work as a team and fuse our powers to recharge the wards. With the lack of added security, the lesser demons had been able to sneak through the cracks.

My uncle was the previous Earth Elementi Warrior, but he died before I ever got to meet him. He had been killed on a mission when I was six years old, but Michael, my older brother, was eighteen months older than me and had worshiped him. What would Michael think if he could see the five of us now? He would've been able to figure out a way to bond us together. I continue to fail every time I try.

My phone vibrated in my pocket and pulled me out of my melancholy thoughts. I looked down to see that it was a text from Micah.

Micah: **Beth has me patrolling with that idiot again**

I sighed. Micah had been my best friend for almost my whole life, but I couldn't understand the animosity between him and Parker.

Me: **It can't be that bad**

Micah: **How would you know? You always get paired up with Hudson or Jay. Why can't you and I just be a team every time and call it good?**

Me: **You know why. If we can't get you and Parker to get along, then there's no hope for our group ever coming together. Also, you hate going on patrol with Hudson and Jay. You need to pull your head out of your ass and deal. The rest of us seem to make it work.**

Micah: **Some fucking help you are.**

I shook my head and put my phone away. If Synergy was really out there and Aiden Ryevick was right about it being human, I didn't envy that person being stuck with this dysfunctional family.

Lailah

The next few days went by smoothly, and I didn't have too many problems getting lost. I made sure that I never went very far from the places I recognized and called Cami if I doubted my surroundings at all. Which, unfortunately, was all the time. Cami was a good sport though, and helped me find my way around. The plan we had set in place the first week worked flawlessly.

It was only week one, and a few of my professors had decided to assign homework on the first day. I was looking over an English assignment at the coffee shop while I waited for Cami, when a shadow fell over my textbook. I assumed she had arrived.

But when I looked up, I saw Brayden instead.

"Hello!" I said, smiling. I was happy to see him again.

"I hope I'm not interrupting," he said, looking from the textbook to me.

"Nope, not at all. I was just glancing over this assignment for one of my classes. Would you like to sit?" I asked, gesturing to the chair across from me.

"Truly, I would love to, but I'm just grabbing a coffee before my Student Council meeting." He gave me an apologetic look.

"No worries, I'm glad you stopped to say hi. Maybe next time we can actually chat," I said, hoping he would agree.

"For sure, maybe we could even plan the next time." He pulled a pen out of his bookbag and wrote his number on my open notebook. "Feel free to text me the next time you're coming here, and I'll try and meet up with you."

Oh. My. God. Did Brayden just give me his number? I nodded, the only answer I could give because I was so nervous that my tongue began to stick to the roof of my mouth.

"Medium latte for Brayden!" the barista called.

"That's me." He turned to go and gave me a parting wave.

I waved back because I didn't know what else to do. Once he was gone, I propped my textbook up on the table and hid my head behind it so I could freak out in privacy. *Could I have been any more awkward? It's not every day that a gorgeous, sweet guy gives me his number. And I couldn't think of one thing to say?*

"Um, hello? You okay back there, Lala?" Cami's voice asked from the other side of my book.

I peeked over the top of it to find her sitting across from me. "How long have you been there?" I asked.

"Long enough to get tired of listening to you mutter to yourself," she retorted. "Wanna tell me what's up?"

"Nothing much. Except one of the hottest guys I've ever met just gave me his phone number," I said, almost hysterical.

Cami reached out with both hands and slammed my textbook closed. "I cannot have this conversation with you while you're hiding behind an English textbook. Now, start at the beginning. Where did we meet this guy?"

"On the grounds tour. When I was with my group, I got distracted and ended up separated from them. I tried to find them again, only to get lost."

"Why am I not shocked?" Cami said, resting her head on her hand and giving me a knowing look.

"Shh! If you're not going to be helpful, no comments from the peanut gallery," I said, frowning.

"I'm sorry, are you calling me small?" she said in mock horror. "Just kidding, I totally resemble that remark, you know, because I'm short and all."

"Anyway," I said, "I ended up by the reflecting pool, and he found me sitting there. He helped get me back to the rest of the group"

"Wait! That's it? He found you and then brought you back to the group? What kind of romance is this? Nope, I'm using my best friend card and vetoing this guy." Cami reached over to rip off the corner of my notebook that had his number on it.

I lunged forward and pulled the notebook away from her. "No, that's not all. He shared his favorite story about that ornate fountain in the reflecting pool. Then, he kept asking me questions and wanted to know more about me. He was so easy to be around." I felt butterflies bouncing around in my stomach.

"So, what's your next move? Are you going to text him, or are you more a talking-on-the-phone kind of gal?" Cami asked, seeming to change her mind about writing this guy off.

"Who says I'm going to do anything about it?" I grumbled.

Cami laughed. "Oh, Lala, you kill me. Of course, you're going to do something about it. Look at you; you're twitterpated for sure."

"I am not!" I said, slapping the notebook back down on the table.

"Oh girl, if I were you, I'd be all over that like a monkey on a cupcake. When was the last time you had your biscuit buttered?" Cami asked, leaning in closer.

"What?" I was totally confused.

"You know! Bumping uglies, a good old slap and tickle, Netflix and chill." Cami raised her brows higher with every phrase. "Wait! Hold the phone! Are you a virgin?"

"No. Well, I don't think so. I've only done it once." I could feel my face burning with embarrassment.

"Okay, let's take this all the way back to the basics. Did he sheath his sword? If the answer is yes, then you are no longer a pure maiden." Cami was grinning at me.

"Yes, he did, and it was awful. I'm not really interested in going through that again." I was shivering at the thought of it.

"I may be more into gal pals, but I do know my fair share about sex. If you hated it that much, then that asshole was doing it all wrong." Cami scooched her chair closer to me. "Now, tell me the whole story with all the ugly gross bits, so I can smash his face in for you."

"His name is Freddy."

"I hate him even more now," Cami said. "Sorry, go on."

"He was on the football team at my high school. We ran into each other all the time because I was on the track team. We trained at the same time after school, the track was around the football field. It was about two months through my freshman year when he started trying to get my attention. He was a junior and one of the best players on the team."

"Scratch that, football makes me despise him more than his name did," Cami cut in.

"Are you going to let me tell this or not?" I snapped, frowning at her.

Cami mimed by zipping her lips closed and tossing away the key. Then she motioned for me to continue.

"He asked me to the homecoming dance for our first date. Of course, I said yes. How many freshmen got the chance to go with an upperclassman who was also on the football team? After that, we dated for about six months. He was charming and funny, of course, he was fit with all the training he did for football. I didn't care for the other guys on the team, but he seemed to be a little more interested in the world outside of football. He would even let me drag him to the museums in Chicago in the spring."

Cami rolled her eyes at this but kept her mouth shut.

"I'm sure you can guess at this point that he asked if we could sleep together. We'd made out, of course, and we had gotten in each other's pants, but never more than heavy petting. My parents had always told my siblings and me about how they waited until marriage. They're so in love, it will make you gag. I always dreamed of having a love like that. Somehow, Freddy had convinced me that sleeping together would deepen our relationship."

Cami laughed, and I did too, thinking of it from Freddy's perspective.

"I finally gave in, and he came up with some lame plan to leave prom early. Freddy had picked a place for us to go afterward. When we got there, I discovered it was a pool house at one of his teammate's houses. He didn't make an effort to make it look nice. There wasn't anything romantic about it, it was just a place we could be alone." I paused and closed my eyes. Now that I was reliving the moment, I realized I'd been an idiot. "I remember thinking I couldn't change my mind because if I did, he would have dumped me for sure. So, I went along with every awkward, painful moment of it. It ended fairly quickly, and he just left, making me think I had done something to make him upset."

Cami's arms wrapped around me, and she hugged me tightly. "I'm so sorry, Lailah."

I could feel my throat begin to tighten, and my eyes stung with tears as I remembered that night. "That's not the worst part," I continued.

"How could it possibly get any worse?" Cami asked, leaning back to look at me.

"It turned out that the only reason he was interested in me was that my two ex-best friends from middle school had spread rumors that I was a slut. Obviously, Freddy realized that this was a lie, but then he made a bet with the football team that he could take my virginity at prom. If those girls hadn't spread those lies, then he never would have taken a second look at me. Needless to say, I spent the rest of my high school days as a "slut," and I was endlessly teased by the whole football team." I brushed away the tears that slipped out.

"Why would anyone do that to you?" Cami demanded.

"One of the girls had a crush on my older brother, and I thought I was being a good friend by telling him about it. When I went back and told her that he was interested in another girl at school, she freaked out on me. They decided that I wasn't good enough to be friends with them, so they cut ties with me after that."

Cami tackled me with her another hug and would've knocked me out of my chair if it wasn't for the wall behind me. "You have me now. I'll never let anything like that happen to you ever again. Any guy that even looks in your direction will have to be vetted by me before they can even talk to you."

I laughed at Cami's protectiveness and soaked up every ounce of it. Meeting her and becoming friends had been a dream come true. "Same goes for me. Any girl who thinks she can just waltz into your life will be cleared with me first. We'll protect each other."

"Preach, sister!" Cami yelled across the café, causing everyone to stare at us. "Now, tell me the name of this mysterious fountain man. I'll need to check him out."

"Actually, you already know him. It's Brayden." I looked at Cami out of the corner of my eye.

Cami paused and looked a little shocked. "Huh."

"What the hell does that mean?" I asked, exasperated.

Cami shrugged her shoulders. "I would just take it slow, no matter who you decide to make a move on. This time though, you'll have me to do some investigating. As for Brayden, he's got a huge white-knight complex, but there could be worse things about a guy."

I grinned because I had experienced his white-knight skills the other day. I mulled over what she said about taking it slow though. It was only the first week of school. There was no need to jump into anything. I looked down at my watch and noticed the time.

"We better get to the dining hall if we want to get dinner before it's all picked over. I really don't want to have another PB&J sandwich," I said, stuffing my school books into my bag.

Seven

Lailah

I should have known better than to expect I could just breeze through the classes at Ryevick. The first week lulled you into thinking things would be easy, but once the second week started, I was hit with project after project. I felt like I was starting to live in the common area of our dorm, just studying my life away. I had gotten into this school on a scholarship, and I needed to prove that they hadn't made a mistake. I wanted to be worthy of the gift they had given me. Cami would come to check on me from time to time, but I was too focused to be bothered for long. This time, Cami came with a bribe.

"Come up for some air, Lala. I brought you one of those god-awful chai lattes," Cami said, holding a cup in front of my face.

"Now, if I remember correctly, you said you'd never order one of these for me," I said, smirking at Cami as I took the cup.

"One of the baristas who knows me took my order, so I wasn't worried he thought it was for me. I also needed to grab a few things in town, so I brought you this." She was holding up a white paper bag.

I recognized the bag from the bakery and grabbed it quickly. I peeked inside to find two sugar cookies. I squealed in excitement and bounced in my seat. I pulled one cookie out and took a bite. I savored the soft, buttery texture with its coating of raw sugar crystals. I let out a low moan of pleasure and ignored the strange looks from a study group across the room

"Geez, Lala. That's the biggest reaction I've gotten out of you all week, and it's over a cookie. You desperately need to get out more if this is setting you off." Cami shook her head in mock concern.

"Forgive me if I'm a little overwhelmed. I got slammed with so many projects this week. I need to add a shirt to my collection that says, 'It's a TRAP!' I can't believe school started only two weeks ago. I wasn't prepared to be flooded with so much work so soon," I said, munching on my cookie.

Cami smiled sympathetically at me. "Okay, I'll let you study to your heart's content tonight, but tomorrow you have to go to a party with me."

"Cami." I groaned. "Chemistry is already kicking my ass. For psych, I have to watch the next part of the case study and make notes on the progress. I also have to finish writing my proposal for my English project, and I have to find a book about the school that is old enough to have information about the original chapel. How can I even justify going to a party?"

"Don't you fret. I've got this all figured out. Watch your case study tonight because it will take the longest. Then we can both look over your chem stuff tomorrow afternoon. That just leaves the book and the English proposal. Do you know what you want to write about?" Cami asked.

"Yes, I have that all planned out," I said, rubbing my forehead. "Where am I supposed to find the book?"

"The school library has a reference section that holds crusty, old history books that can't leave the building. There has to be one in there that would work."

I was running out of reasons not to go to this party. She had basically planned out my study needs perfectly. "Are you even any good at chemistry?"

"I'm better than you are. I took that same class last year. How different could it be?" Cami asked, shrugging her shoulders.

"You took Organic Chemistry your first year too? I was told by everyone it was a stupid choice." I was surprised, since I knew Cami wanted to be an English major.

"What the fucking hell, Lala!? Who takes Organic Chem in their first year? No wonder the class is kicking your ass! Forget what I said! I can't help you with that shit! I barely made it through Intro to Chem!" Cami exclaimed as she almost fell out of her chair. "Christ! You're even doing that class while taking three others? Are you asking for college suicide in your first semester?"

I grabbed Cami and covered her mouth with my hands, trying to get her to shut up before we got kicked out of the room. "I tested out of doing an intro class, so I had to pick a higher level, and this one sounded more interesting than the others."

When I didn't let go of her, she licked the inside of my hand and got the desired effect of me releasing her as quickly as possible. "Very mature."

"It's official. I'm dragging you to that party whether you like it or not. You need to live a little. Be a real college student. Everyone fails a course at some point and has to take it over again. It's part of the experience."

"How come I didn't read about it in the brochure?" I grumbled. "You don't understand. My brother graduated top of his class at Notre Dame, so I have to do well here."

Cami grabbed my shoulders and looked deep into my eyes, freaking me out a little. "I bet if I called your parents right now and told them that you haven't seen the light of day all week, except to go to class and eat, they would tell you the same thing I am. Enjoy the experience. Try new things. What happened to the girl who told me she wanted to live the college dream? Going to a college party is the pinnacle of being an official student."

"Okay, you can tone down the theatrics. I'll go," I relented.

"Whoop whoop! It's time to jam out with my clam out," Cami said, throwing a good fist pump into the air as she got up to leave.

I shook my head as she left me to my studies. I wasn't going to have a chance to worm my way out of this now that I had said I would go. I smiled as I pulled my laptop out to watch the video for psych. *What should U wear,* I wondered, *I've never gone to a party before.*

Saturday passed in a blur of studying. Cami kept me on task to make sure I finished everything. When it came time to get ready for the party, Cami came up to my room because she decided I needed help. I really couldn't argue with her. She had laughed at me when I showed her the five things of makeup that I had. When I opened the door for her to come in, she had so much stuff that I thought she was moving in, not just helping me get ready for a party.

I took in Cami's outfit and suddenly got worried. She was wearing a bright-pink crop top with a cropped black mesh top over it. Her black jean shorts were very short, but they came up higher on the waist. Her makeup was flawless, and her eyeshadow looked like a sunset had burst from them. I hoped to God that she didn't think I was going to dress like that tonight.

"Take a deep breath, Lala. I'm not going to Cami-fy you. I don't think you could handle the power a look like this would give you," she said, giggling at the panic I was sure was written all over my face. "You're way too girl-next-door. We just need to pump up the natural look that you've got going on."

I sighed in relief. She walked over to prop a mirror on my desk and motioned for me to sit in front of it. "First, we need to tackle that outrageous head of hair that you have. I hope Pinterest doesn't fail me now."

I sat down in the chair and pulled the scrunchie out of my hair, releasing the beast in all its wild glory. I watched intently as Cami took my spray-in conditioner, misted my whole head, and dove in. Taking more time than I ever would, she spritzed and scrunched my curls until she molded them into the shape she wanted. When she was done, I was amazed at how sleek it looked compared to the frizzy puff that I always managed.

"Hell yeah! God, I'm good. Maybe I need to change my career path and go into the hair taming business," Cami said, clapping excitedly at her handy work.

"Cami, this is amazing. Seriously, I've never been able to get it to look this good," I gushed, turning to and fro in the mirror.

"Now, for my next trick, I will turn your beautiful face into a look that would stop a bus in its tracks," Cami said as she rummaged through the bags she brought.

She piled a ton of products I was unfamiliar with on the desk. I tried not to flinch as she applied all of it to my face. She kept turning me away so I couldn't catch a glimpse of myself in the mirror. Finally, when she was done, I got to see the final masterpiece. I blinked a few times, unsure that it was really me looking back. A girl—no, a woman—stared back at me with bright, fresh skin and crystal-blue eyes that popped. She had even put on a soft-pink lipstick that made my lips look much fuller than I could ever remember them being.

"Holy shit!" was all I managed to say.

Cami bounced around the room, singing her own praises to Elle the elephant, who was sitting on my bed. "Why, thank you, Elle. It's my best work if I do say so myself. Oh, you're too kind. Stop, please. I'm blushing."

"I picked out two outfits, but you'll have to tell me which one works—or not," I said, walking over to my coffee table where I had set them out.

Cami walked over and looked them over; one was a simple black dress that was knee length and had cap sleeves. The other was a pair of skinny jeans with some distressing on the knees and a slouchy, off-the-shoulder, light-blue shirt.

"If you're willing to give it a try, I have a shirt that would go with these jeans perfectly." She pulled said shirt out from another of her bags.

"I'm not sure you and I are the same size on top. I might stretch it out," I said sheepishly.

"It's fine. You can say your chi-chis are bigger than mine. I'm very happy with my little handfuls." She handed me the emerald shirt.

I shimmied into the pants and pulled the shirt over my head. I was surprised to find it fit perfectly. It was off the shoulder and skintight, but the sleeves went to my elbows, so I didn't feel exposed.

"Wow, you had this?" I said, looking in the mirror she brought. The green set off my fair skin and made my blonde hair shine.

"I might have gone into town and bought the shirt for you to wear tonight," Cami said. I turned to scold her, but she raised her hands, stopping me. "I knew that this was your first party, and I wanted it to be perfect. I couldn't in good conscience let you wear anything that you already own."

I frowned, but I wasn't sure if I was more bothered by the fact that she went shopping for me, or that she didn't like any of my clothes.

"Don't get me wrong. I live for your T-shirt collection. That one the other day that said 'Shhh, no one cares' was priceless. I love that you don't need fancy clothes to be who you are, but every once in a while, every girl needs some new clothes."

I had to agree with her. The shirt was amazing, and something that I never would have tried on, but I loved it. "Thank you, Cami. It means a lot that you care so much to make this night awesome."

"Aw, of course, you're my girl. Now it's time for me to get ready for this thing," Cami said. When I paused at what she said to look at her, she started laughing. "Oh man, I had you for a minute."

The party was being hosted at a student housing complex off-campus. Apparently, Ryevick had a strict policy about parties on school grounds. The students had quickly figured out a way around that, and truthfully, I think the school was quite aware of what was going on. When we arrived in Cami's car, the party was well underway. I had asked Cami why we didn't start getting ready till eight, but she informed me that the party didn't really get going until eleven. She told me it was embarrassing to show up too early, but she took into consideration that it was my first party, and we got there at nine-thirty.

The house was a beacon in the dark night. Loud music could be heard thumping as we drove up the country road where it was located. When we walked up, tons of students were milling about on a large wrap-around porch with drinks in their hands. The front door was wide open, so we just walked in. The living room was filled with people chatting, making out, and playing what looked like poker at the dining room table. I followed Cami into the kitchen, where food was spread out on the counter, along with three kegs of beer.

"Cami, I wondered if you would be gracing us with your presence at the first party of the year," a busty redhead greeted her and kissed Cami on both cheeks.

"Once I heard it was one of yours, Maggs, I couldn't refuse. This is my friend Lailah; she's a freshman," Cami said.

Maggs nodded her head at me and looked me over with a critical eye. "What can I get you ladies to drink?" she asked, apparently satisfied with what she saw. "I have a dark, amber, or cider for those of us that are gluten-free."

"I would love the amber, and Lailah should probably have a cider," Cami said, giving me a look over her shoulder. "I'm guessin' you're not much of a drinker?"

"You would be correct on that, but it's because in the states we can't drink till we're twenty-one, and that's still a few months away." I didn't want to appear lame in front of Maggs.

They both shrugged and seemed to accept that explanation as Maggs handed over our drinks. "You guarding the goods all night, or are one of the other girls going to take over for you later?" Cami asked.

"Not tonight. I have to set the newbies straight on how my parties roll," Maggs said, winking at us. "Go have fun. We opened up the backyard because it's still nice out."

Taking her cue, we headed outside onto the patio. There was a ping pong table set up for beer pong, and it looked like there was quite an intense game going on. Squealing from across the yard caught my attention, and I saw a hot tub filled with people. The water was sloshing over the sides like a tidal wave had hit.

I looked over to say something to Cami, but she was talking to another girl I didn't know. I caught her eye and motioned that I was going to sit on one of the patio chairs. She nodded and gave me a smile with a wink of encouragement.

I sipped on my drink and was surprised when I discovered that I really liked it. It was sweet and yet had enough of a bite to it that I knew it was for adults. My eyes wandered over the crowd of people dancing in the grass where the DJ was set up. Some danced in groups enjoying the flow of the music, while others looked like they might as well just be having sex; it would actually have been less provocative.

Before I knew it, I was done with my drink. I scanned the patio to see if I could find Cami to let her know that I was going to get a refill, but couldn't see her. *How lost can I get in a house,* I thought. *I feel like I can manage this on my own.* I made my way back toward the kitchen, grabbing a few snacks along the way.

"Ready for another?" Maggs asked, holding out the hose for the keg.

"Yeah, thanks, this is really an awesome party," I said and found I really meant it.

"You're welcome. I've found it's my calling in life to provide a place for people to let loose while in the throes of college life. Some students get so caught up in the schoolwork, they forget to live in the moment. Don't you agree?" she asked, raising an eyebrow.

I laughed. No wonder Cami liked this woman, they were kindred spirits. "I would be one of those people if not for Cami." I nodded my thanks and headed back out to the patio.

On my way out, I ran into a group of guys walking in. I almost spilled my drink all over one of them. "I'm so sorry, I hope I didn't get any on you," I said, looking him over.

"I wouldn't have minded if you had, then you could have helped me clean off," the guy said, giving me a sly grin.

I groaned internally. *Please, no; please don't let this be happening to me. I was having such a nice time.*

"Thankfully, crisis averted, and there's nothing to clean." I tried to brush past him, but his friends blocked my way.

"I'm Max, by the way," he said, holding out his hand.

I shook it quickly before pulling my hand back not wanting to get trapped. "Lailah."

"Oh, you're scholarship girl. Damn, who knew someone from the states could pull that off? Smart and sexy, what an enticing duo." He was trying to be charming but failing.

"Thanks, I was pretty surprised to get the scholarship too, I fully expected to be rejected." *Ha, what are you going to say to that, idiot?*

"Did you send a picture along with your application? I know they try to have diversity, and we are on short supply of doe-eyed Yankees," Max said.

"Excuse me?" I snapped. Was this guy trying to be an asshole or was this his poor attempt at charming? He was strongly leaning in the asshole direction. "First, Americans do not find that term endearing. Second, if you're trying to pick up a girl, don't call her a derogatory slur. It pisses us off and makes you look like a douchebag."

"What the fuck," Max said, towering over me.

Oh God, how I wanted to run away from this fight, but my big mouth started it. What was wrong with me? I'd never started a fight; sure, I'd dreamed about stepping up for myself and telling people what I thought all the time, but it never really happened.

"Look, bitch, I was just trying to be friendly, no need to get all high and mighty. Maybe you were right, and you shouldn't be at this school." His friends now started to close in on me.

"Lailah! Why didn't you text me and tell me you were here?" Parker said, appearing out of nowhere putting his arm around my shoulders. "Hey, Max, have you met my friend, Lailah?"

"Actually, we did meet, and I was just about to excuse myself to look for you." I played along with Parker's ruse.

"Here I am, no need to look any further. See ya later, Max," Parker said as he turned us around and headed through the house and upstairs.

"Where are you taking me?" I said, worried I had jumped from one problem to another.

"There's a small deck up here that not many people know about. I figured you might want a little space from the party, and it gives Max a chance to chill the fuck out." He opened a set of French doors to a wrought iron patio with two large deck chairs piled with pillows.

"Is this where you take all the girls you rescue at parties?" I teased, settling into one of the chairs.

"To be honest, I think you're the first person I've brought up here. Typically, I chill up here alone when I need a breather." Parker stared out over the lawn filled with people.

I looked at Parker with a different lens. I never would've guessed that he would need a breather from people. He seemed to thrive on the interactions with others, but maybe everyone needs a moment to themselves.

"Thank you for getting me out of there." I turned to watch the party and took a sip from my drink. "I don't know what came over me, I never get in people's faces like that."

"I think it might be your drink loosening your tongue and lowering your normal censoring ability." Parker chuckled. "Either way, I'm happy to help, but you didn't look like you were doing too badly on your own. Max is an idiot when it comes to hot girls, he always manages to piss them off. You were kind enough to tell him why he pissed you off, most just walk away."

"I'm glad to know I'm not epically failing at my first party." I took a gulp of my drink.

"This is your first college party or first party ever?" Parker leaned his elbows on his knees.

I blushed under his focused attention. "Ever. I never got invited to any in high school, and with my town being so small, I didn't want to spend extra time with any of those people."

Parker shot to his feet and reached out to me. "Come on, if this is your first party, there is no way I'm letting you stay up here. You need to get the full experience; finish your drink, and we'll get in on the next beer pong game."

"Nope, not gonna happen, there's no way I can go from not drinking ever to a game of beer pong." I shook my head vigorously.

"Fine, I'll drink all the beer, but you're going to play with me," Parker said, reaching down and grabbing my hand. "Trust me, this is going to be a night to remember."

"I am so going to regret this tomorrow. I just know it." I let Parker tug me back downstairs.

We managed to get in the next game of beer pong fairly quickly, and Parker explained the rules for me. "You're going to toss the ball into the cup; when you do, they need to drink it. The same happens in reverse when they have a ball land in one of our cups. I had three of the cups filled with hard cider, so you have to do those, I'll do the rest." Parker was grinning.

We managed to win, even though I sucked at the game. I managed to get the ball in the cup twice, much to Parker's delight. I ended up having to drink two of the three cups of cider. By the time we finished the game, my whole body felt warm and tingly all over.

At some point, Cami appeared by my side to check in on me. "You good, Lala? I just want to make sure that moron isn't pushing you too far."

"I love you for checking in on me, but I'm actually having a great time!" I said, grabbing her into a hug. "What about you? Are you having fun? Did you find a cute girl to hang out with?"

Cami smiled and shook her head at me. "Lala, tipsy is a good look for you. I knew somewhere in that perfect outer shell there was a wild child hidden."

"Lailah, come on; now, we have to go get our groove on," Parker said, grabbing my hand again waving to Cami. "You coming, half-pint?"

"What did you call me, asshat?" Cami said, laughing as she followed after us.

"I have no idea how to dance!" I yelled over the pulsing music.

"You don't have to, just let the music move you," Cami said. "Close your eyes, and just let your body figure it out."

Taking a deep breath, I took her advice and closed my eyes, letting the music flow across my skin. I danced all the time at home while I cleaned, or Kyle and I would have dance-off battles with video games, but never something like this. A song I knew came on next, and I started to relax into it, singing along and swaying. The song was remixed and moved with a slightly faster beat that just pulled my body along. I opened my eyes and found that I'd drifted further into the mob of gyrating people. I looked around to see if I could find Cami. She was off having some dance battle with another guy, and they could both dance crazy good. Then I felt someone behind me, I stiffened when the person put their hands on my hips gently. They didn't crowd me but just guided me along with the beat. I looked over my shoulder and saw that it was Parker.

"I hope you don't mind. A few guys were on their way over to make a move, and I figured I might be the lesser of evils," Parker said into my ear.

Someone bumped into us and caused him to pull me against him, so I wouldn't fall. We both paused a moment, unsure of what to do next. Parker loosened his hold, letting me move away if I wanted. I'm not sure if it was the alcohol or the fact that Parker felt safe to me, I leaned back against him and let him lead. One song flowed into another, and Parker and I spent the rest of the night on the dance floor. Cami came to join us with another girl, and we showed off every bad dance move we all knew. Utterly exhausted and dying of thirst, I had to get something to drink. I grabbed Cami and forced our way out of the crowd. We burst out of the people, laughing when a girl ran into me, spilling her full beer all over me.

"Better watch where you're going, charity case, wouldn't want to ruin too many clothes," the girl who ran into me said, flipping her hair over her shoulder and walking off.

"What the hell is her problem?" I grumbled, wiping at my shirt. My happy buzz was officially killed now that I was covered in warm beer.

"What a twat-a-potamus; she should be watching where she's going," Cami yelled after the girl.

Parker emerged out of the dancing mass and walked over once he spotted us. "What happened? You okay?"

"I'm fine, but some bimbo just spilled her beer all over me," I explained. "Looks like we'll have to head back. I'm not spending the rest of the night in wet jeans."

"You also smell like a homeless drunk," Cami said as she leaned in and sniffed me.

"Gee, thanks," I said, rolling my eyes.

"Are you guys going to be okay getting home?" Parker asked, looking at Cami.

"Yup, I only had one drink when we first got here. Tonight was all about Lala getting the full experience, and that includes a hangover tomorrow." Cami gave me a thumbs up.

"That is a horrible thing to do to your best friend," I scolded her.

Parker just grinned, watching our interaction. "Sounds like you're in good hands to me, Trouble."

"Trouble is the opposite of what I normally am," I said defiantly.

Cami coughed, trying to cover her laughter at that statement. "Yeah, says the girl who ends up in trouble whenever unsupervised."

"Whatever," I said, waving a dismissing hand. "Thank you, Parker, for forcing me to have fun. I actually ended up having a blast."

"Give me your phone," Parker said, holding out his hand.

I reached into my back pocket and pulled it out, handing it to him. He then proceeded to add his number into my contacts and handed it back over. "You really should put a lock on your phone, you never know who might be slipping their number in."

I bit my lip at his scolding since Cami also was on my case about why I didn't lock it. "I'll keep that in mind."

Parker gave me a side hug since I was still covered in beer, and we made our way back to where Cami had parked.

"Look at you, ya little player! Two numbers in almost as many weeks; I'd say you're on a roll," Cami teased as we drove back to Ashfall.

"He really is very sweet, he's like a big teddy bear that just wants to have fun." I smiled, remembering his body against mine. He definitely wasn't fluffy like a teddy bear; nope, that was solid muscle I felt.

Cami helped me to my room, and I fell into my bed like it was going to save me from the shifting ground beneath my feet. I felt her pulling off my shoes, but I didn't manage to stay awake long enough to hear her leave. Darkness enveloped me, but it wasn't the blissful void of sleep. No, this was something different, I felt afraid of this black world. It seemed that I had fallen into one of those dreams where some unknown evil was chasing me, and it was all I could do to keep running. The danger was closing in on me, claws catching in my hair—

"You have a new text message!"

My phone notification cut through the darkness and pulled me out of my nightmare. I groped around to find my phone and looked at it with one eye. It was Parker making sure I'd gotten back okay. Letting the phone drop, I rolled over, and this time when I shut my eyes, I was blessed with a dreamless sleep.

Eight

Lailah

On Sunday, I didn't get anything done. I stayed in bed and felt like I died slowly. Cami took pity on me and brought me food and ibuprofen to help with the pounding headache. I think I drank a gallon of Gatorade and still felt like I was run over by a Mack truck. I tried to work on my chemistry homework, but I just couldn't focus on the words in the textbook, so I gave up. Cami brought up her laptop, and we watched America's Next Top Model and ate junk food all afternoon.

Thankfully by Monday, I was back to normal, except for a lingering headache. I vowed that I was never going to drink again—the aftermath was so not worth the buzz. Cami met me in the lobby so we could eat breakfast together before she walked me to my University 101 class. I was starting to figure out where things were, but I didn't trust myself quite yet. Cami didn't mind, because any time I had her up before ten, I bought her coffee.

"You have a test in your chem class today, right?" Cami asked as we bussed our trays.

"She called it a quiz, but she made them all worth ten points each in the class. Professor Lark didn't tell us how many there were either, saying that *surprises were the spice of life.*" I groaned.

"That's just plain evil," Cami said, linking her arm with mine as we walked to class.

"Oh yeah, I need to go to the library tonight after classes so I can look for that book you were telling me about," I said.

"I have a family dinner tonight with my sisters, but I can come get you after I'm done if that works for you. That is, if you think you can find your way to the library on your own," Cami teased.

"There are enough people on campus that I can stop and ask directions from if I need to. The map you made me really helps, though; you should add that to your skills. Cami: specialty map maker for the directionally challenged," I said as if I were reading it off a blinking street sign. "What is your last name? I should make sure they spell it right in the headlines."

"It's Whittemore," Cami said offhandedly.

"Any relation to my psych teacher? Her last name is Whittemore, too," I said jokingly.

Cami didn't answer right away, so I stopped and looked down at her. "She's my older sister; she's one of the sisters I'm having dinner with tonight."

"Seriously," I said, shocked. "I was totally kidding when I asked that."

"Yeah, I don't like to talk about it much; people get weird when they know you're related to a professor," Cami said, shrugging. "Top that off with the fact that I grew up with the five guys that live in The Manor, and I make a lot of fake friends who just want something from me."

"Except me, I couldn't care less that you have a sister who teaches here, and I don't really feel the need to use you to get to those five guys," I pointed out.

"No, you seem to be doing just fine with that on your own." Cami laughed, breaking the tension. "Come on, wouldn't want you to be late for your ever-so-interesting *freshman* class."

"You know you love all the stories I tell you. I can see the way you perk up whenever I talk about that branch-off group from the Knights Templar. I wonder if I can find more about the Elementi when I'm looking up stuff about the chapel," I mused as we arrived at the building my class was in.

"Only one way to find out. Text me when you're done at the library, and I'll come get you. You'll be the perfect excuse if I need to leave dinner early," Cami said, shoving me through the door.

My University 101 class flew by; we all spent the class researching our part of school history that we had picked out the week before. I'd been intrigued by Ryevick's bypassing of the church's ruling by creating the chapel. I was also curious to figure out why the church felt the need to monitor what the artist produced. When the class ended, I walked up to Professor Phillips.

"Do you have a moment?" I asked.

"Of course, Lailah, what can I do for you," he asked, setting down a stack of papers.

"I picked the chapel to research, and I just wanted to know if our library had books about it," I inquired, not wanting to waste my night looking for something that wasn't there.

Professor Phillips paused, scratching his chin. "Yes, I do believe it should. It will be in the far back reference room. You need teacher permission to have access to those books since they're one of a kind and very old. Let me write you a note that you can give to the librarian. They should let you in no problem."

"Oh," I said, surprised that there would be such guarded books at the school. I should have known better though, this school was all about preserving its history. "Would this section also have any information on the Elementi?"

Professor Phillips paused in his writing and looked up at me, with a raised eyebrow. "Now, why would you want to know more about that?"

"I'm a huge sucker for history and a lover of fantasy. I feel like with what little you mentioned about it, it sounds like a wonderful combination of both those things. I just figured if I was already back there, I might take the opportunity to find out more." I was feeling shy at admitting my curious mind.

"If there is anything more about them, that would be one of the only places available for you to find something," Professor Phillips said a little cryptically, handing me the note for the librarian.

"Thank you, I really appreciate it," I said, bobbing my head in thanks.

I looked down at my watch and realized I was running behind for my psych class. I hurried down the hall and took the covered walkway across to the other building. I managed to slip in a few minutes late but didn't draw any attention to myself. Professor Whittemore was typing away at her computer, pulling up the slides we would be going over today in class. I looked at her with new eyes knowing that she was Cami's sister.

Nona Whittemore was just slightly taller than Cami; they had the same bright-green eyes, but Nona wore large round glasses. I bet if Cami didn't bleach her hair white, it would be the same honey-brown color as Nona's. For as much as Cami cared for her appearance, Nona did not; her clothes were rumpled and looked like they might have been slept in.

"Okay, class. Today we'll be going over the study we've been following. Have any of you figured out the objective they settled on for this experiment?" Professor Whittemore asked.

"They're doing a study on lying," one student called out.

When she didn't react to that answer, others started to call out their ideas as well.

"It's about cheating to get ahead."

"No, I think it's about how lying can get you places, what power it can give you."

"No, that was the original objective, but it changed once they got started."

Professor Whittemore held up her hand at this last guess, cutting off the rest of the answers. "You are correct in the fact that they started out with one objective, some of you named elements of it, but failed to grasp the whole idea."

While the rest of the students murmured amongst themselves, I went over the notes on the videos; then I saw it. Underlined in my notes, I saw the answer Professor Whittemore was looking for. I had been so intrigued by the idea that I made a note of it. Taking a deep breath, I raised my hand and waited for her to notice. She looked up at me, pushing her glasses up her nose and gave a little smirk, or at least I thought it was one before her face went neutral again.

"You think you know the answer?" she called out to me.

I nodded my head, and she motioned for me to go ahead. "The study started out about lying to get ahead, but when they got further into the study, they decided they cared more about why they lied. What drove them to use that tactic to get what they wanted. They wanted to understand the human brain and what effect it had on it when they lied."

Professor Whittemore clapped her hands once, leaping back to her desk in excitement. "Yes! These scientists and psychologists wanted to know what lying did to the human brain."

She flipped to the first slide and started going into the chemical changes that happened when someone lied. I was riveted, seeing how something we all do without even realizing it changed the way we thought and what was real. Some people lied so much that their lies became a reality to them. Others, in extreme cases, got sick over the guilt of lying, unable to keep the truth hidden. Some said that when they lied, it felt like they were hypnotized or possessed into saying it. Overall, I was pumped to follow this case study.

Once psych was over, I had enough time to head to the coffee shop and get a pick-me-up chai before my Organic Chem class. I passed a bulletin board that had ads all over it for tutors in various subjects. I looked over all of them and was shocked at the price of a one-hour session. *Do all tutors charge? Does the school have any on staff who will help struggling students?* I chewed on my lip absently while I looked over the board one more time to see if I missed any.

"Would you look at that? The charity case is getting overwhelmed and needs help. Too bad, she can't afford it," a girl walking out said to a friend.

"Maybe she should have picked an easier school to go to; elite schools are for elite students," her friend responded.

I tried to shake it off as I walked up to the counter to order my drink. Clearly, it didn't work because the barista gave me a sympathetic look. "Don't mind them. They get catty any time one of The Manor boys takes an interest in a girl. It will stop once they move on to someone else."

"That's stupid, I didn't ask for them to talk to me," I complained. "What gives them the right to get upset anyway? Why don't they make an effort to get to know the guys instead of torturing innocent people like me?"

The barista just shrugged her shoulders, probably wishing she'd never said anything to me. I collected my chai and rushed off to class. I wanted to get there and go over my class notes to refresh my brain on the information before the quiz. I found a seat, pulled out my books, and glanced at the syllabus, making sure I was looking over the right section. I knew this quiz would tell me if I was going to need to bite the bullet and get a tutor or not. Before I knew it, I looked up, and the classroom was full, and it was time.

Professor Lark had her TA pass out the quiz for us while she went over the importance of them again. "These quizzes are not to be taken lightly. They can make or break your grade. Fail two of these, and you might make it; fail three or more, and you can kiss your GPA goodbye. Good luck, and when you finish the quiz, bring it up front and leave it in my box. My TA, Hudson, will be watching over you. I have learned my classes do better when I'm not present for the test-taking."

I could feel the sweat starting to bead on my forehead. I could not fuck this up, I needed to pass this class with a B+ or higher. When Hudson reached me, he handed me my sheet and gave me an encouraging smile. I tried to smile back, but I was pretty sure I had failed. I grabbed my pencil and stared at the quiz. It was only twenty questions; I could manage this.

As I went from question to question, I started to second-guess myself at every turn. I would mark one bubble, then erase it and try again. When I was finally down to the last three questions, someone cleared their throat above me. I looked up to find Hudson standing next to me.

"I just wanted to make sure you knew there were only five minutes left for the class," he informed me.

I looked around, and I was the only person left in the classroom, everyone else had finished and left. *Are you kidding me? It has taken me almost an hour to do this stupid twenty-question quiz!*

"Thanks for the heads-up, I'll be done in time." I returned to my test, randomly picking the answers to the last two questions.

I collected my things and walked quickly up to the front and dropped my test off in the box. I gave Hudson a small smile and bolted out of the room, humiliated that I had taken so long over a simple quiz. *God, could I have looked any more stupid?*

Done with classes for the day, I headed to the cafeteria on the main campus that had simple pre-made foods. I was so thankful that my scholarship covered everything—even the food. I just had to let them scan the special card they sent me, and it was taken care of. I grabbed a turkey sandwich and headed to the open seating. The routine Cami and I had fallen into was meeting here to do homework we didn't want to suffer through alone. I glanced down at my watch and saw it was already past four. I was surprised that she wasn't already here waiting for me. I texted her just in case she had lost track of time.

> Me: **Hey, I'm at the cafeteria if you want to join me**

Not wanting to give anyone an excuse to come pester me, I pulled out my school books. I started on my psych homework since I was excited about that. After that embarrassing moment with the quiz, I was going to need something fun. Lost in my work, I didn't notice how much time had passed. When I looked outside, the sun was already setting, and the students were now eating dinner. I looked at my phone surprised that Cami hadn't called me. Sure enough, my phone had been on silent, and I didn't notice her texts come through.

> Cami: **My sisters decided they wanted to make a night out of it, so we went into town.**

> Cami: **Sorry, I forgot to text you sooner.**

> Cami: **Please don't be mad at me. I LOVE YOU!**

Apparently, she hadn't taken my silence well.

Me: **I'm not mad, calm down, I left my phone on silent and didn't see them until now.**

Cami: **DON'T DO THAT TO ME!!!!!!! Text me if you need anything, you know it won't take me long to drive back.**

I smiled, knowing Cami would love the excuse to drive like a bat out of hell to come to my aid.

Me: **I'll be fine, I have to learn how to do this on my own sometime.**

Cami: **My baby's all grown up!**

I grabbed a power bar to eat later while I searched through the library. Now would be the perfect time to go since everyone would be at dinner, and I could find a good spot to camp out. I pulled out my map for dummies that Cami made me, with everything written in landmark references that I would understand. Lucky me, the library was close by, just behind the building I took claculus in. I headed off, confident I could manage the rest of the night on my own.

I managed to find the library with ease. I mentally patted myself on the back for a job well done. I pushed open the heavy wooden doors to the hush of the world within. I loved how reverent every library was, the hushed tones of people, the smell of books, and the calm that came over you in the silent world.

I walked up to the information desk in the front of the lobby area. "Hello, I'm looking for a book in the reference library."

"Do you have written permission from a teacher?" the woman asked, peering over her computer at me.

I pulled the note out and handed it to her. The woman slipped on a pair of glasses and read over the note. Then she picked up the phone and spoke softly into it. "Someone will be with you shortly to escort you into the room," she said, looking back at me.

"Thank you," I said, thrown off by all this extra effort for a room full of books.

I looked over at the section of books by the front door. Moments later, an older man walked up to me in his loafers and a Mr. Rogers cardigan.

"Are you looking to get into the special archives?" he asked.

"I think so. Mr. Phillips gave me a note for the reference section. Is that the same thing?" I asked.

"Hmm, I see. Follow me then," he said and walked away.

I trailed after him, even more curious to see what could be stored in the special archives. We walked to the very back of the library and down a short hall. At the end of the hall, a metal accordion gate blocked the way to the room beyond. There was a soft glow emitting from the room, making it seem like something out of Harry Potter.

The gentleman pulled an old iron skeleton key out of his pocket and opened the gate for me. "You will have one hour to use the books; no food, no drinks, and no flashes are to be used on or near the books. These are priceless archives that are irreplaceable. Handle them with care."

I nodded my agreement to the instructions. "I understand. I will be very careful with the books."

"I will be back in an hour to let you out, unless you are done sooner. In which case, there is a phone in the room that connects to the front desk. Let them know you're done, and I will let you out," he said, frowning at me as if he wasn't sure he should let me into the room.

I walked into the room, and he pulled the gate closed behind me, locking it. It made me wonder if, at some point, kids had gotten permission to be here and let others in who weren't supposed to be. I looked around the room, unsure of where to start. Everything in the room was made of dark glossy wood that made the room feel comforting. There were two levels to check out, and I was so drawn to the metal wraparound staircase, I couldn't help but start on the top floor.

Once on the second floor, I looked at the shelves to see if they were labeled. Plaques on the top section of the bookcase provided guidance as to what each column held. The columns were ordered by date, dating back to the twelfth century. I worked my way around to the sixteen hundreds until I could find the right year. Finally locating the appropriate area, I started to look through the books to find something that would help in my research. I found logbooks from different artists at the time, filled with clients and commissions. Finally, I found a book filled with letters going back and forth with the builders of the chapel.

I sat down on the floor, resting against the wrought iron railing, flipping through the letters. Although super interesting, I didn't find anything that I could use for my project. Slipping the book back on the shelf, I tried a few others, getting some good information that I copied down in my notebook. I checked the next few years to see if there was anything I could use but decided I had gotten all the history on the subject these books held. I then decided to look at what they could possibly have dated back to the twelfth century.

I found documentation of major events during the time Renaissance art was on the rise, medieval universities were being founded, and the Knights Templar were founded. I continued to pick randomly from the section, since so many fascinating things happened during this time in history. Then I picked up a book on the Knights Templar and their history.

As I was flipping through, I stumbled upon the first mention of the Elementi I'd seen. The passage briefly mentioned that it was a branch of the Templars after the Battle of Hattin, during the decline of the Knights.

I googled the date of the battle and scanned the books to find something closer to that time. I pulled a few books that looked promising, but they were much older than what I'd been reading before and were hard to read in the soft lighting. I looked at the lower floor and found a couch with a lamp next to it. I noticed it was darker in the lower section as I hurried down the steps and over to the couch. I set the stack of books gently on the coffee table and grabbed the top one to start on first. I was so excited, I flopped onto the couch, and instead of landing on the couch cushion, I landed on a person. Before I could stand up, I was already in motion toward the floor.

"What the fuck?! Don't you look before you decide to sit on someone?" a male voice said as he pushed me off him.

Unable to think fast enough, I thumped to the floor in a heap, slapping myself in the face with the book. "I'm so sorry, I didn't know anyone else was in here!" I looked up, rubbing my nose to find angry sapphire eyes glaring at me.

"Who the hell are you, and what are you doing here?" he barked.

I looked at him wide-eyed, shocked by the angry words directed at me. His long dark brown hair was all mussed from laying on the couch, making it stand up in all different directions. He was handsome to be sure, even with the scowl scrunching up his face. His deep-blue eyes seemed to sear right into me as he waited for my answer. The contrast of his overbearing demeanor to his wild hairstyle struck something inside me, and I couldn't help but laugh. That reaction caught him off guard. He frowned deeper at me, swinging his feet off the couch so he was sitting directly in front of me and leaning close enough I could feel his warm breath on my skin.

"What the hell are you laughing at? Do you have any idea what deep shit you're in right now?" he demanded, trying to intimidate me. "How the hell did you even get into this room?"

"I'm sorry, I truly am. I didn't mean to laugh, it's just this whole situation caught me off guard, and to see you so angry, and your hair," I said, gesturing to his head. "It just struck me as funny, and I couldn't help myself," I said, wiping my eyes with my sleeve. I laughed so hard I had teared up.

"Are you mental?" he asked, combing his fingers through his hair and trapping it away in a man bun.

"I don't think so," I said, still unsure how to handle this whole situation. "Wait! How long have you been in this room? The man who let me in here didn't tell me that anyone else was here," I challenged.

"It doesn't matter how I got in. Why are you here?" he asked, waving off my question.

"I got permission from one of my teachers to be here. I'm going to assume that you didn't, or why else would you be hiding on the couch?" I said, pointing a finger in his face.

"I wasn't hiding, I was napping. There's a difference. Whatever. I don't need to justify myself to you or anyone else. Just make sure you look before you sit on someone else." He knocked my hand out of his way as he stood up. "What an idiot."

"What did you call me?" I snapped, clambering to my feet. "Why am *I* an idiot for sitting on a couch in a dark room, when *you're* the one sleeping in the middle of the library!"

"Who jumps on a couch like a little kid? Only an idiot wouldn't turn the light on in a room this dark to make sure they didn't sit on something. It's only logical," he said, glaring at me before he turned and started walking away again.

Normally, things like this wouldn't bother me. I always let stuff like this roll off, not wanting conflict. Yet, for some reason, there was something about this guy that set my emotions on overdrive. It was as if he'd shocked me into action, and I could feel emotions building up inside me. *How dare he treat me like I'm some bug on his shoe! I apologized for sitting on him, he doesn't have to be a dick about it.*

I watched him walk across the room to a door I hadn't seen before. While I was glaring at him, I felt my anger slowly fade as my brain absorbed the drool-worthy body he had. I'd never been one to check out a dude, but I think it's because I hadn't seen anyone with such a great ass before. Letting my gaze wander up past his muscular ass, I noticed the snug T-shirt that showed off his toned back. My hands clenched with a desire to run them across his skin to make sure what I saw was real. My train of thought came to a screeching halt when I realized he'd stopped and looked back at me from the door, catching me checking him out. His face grimaced at me as if my appreciation of him was unwelcome. Saying nothing, he pulled open the door and left, heading outside.

"Well, that couldn't have been any worse," I muttered to the empty room.

Nine

Micah

I never thought the day would come that we truly would have all six of us together. I knew the stories and the history we were taught, but I never really believed that the sixth element was real.

I stopped in the path outside the library and punched the wall to my right. I took my hand away to see I'd cracked the stone and the skin on my hand. *Why did it have to be a woman? None of the five before us had ever been female. It always passed to a male of the family line. How can we do our jobs if we're worried about some silly woman who was clueless enough to sit on me?* I punched the wall again, this time knocking off a chunk of stone as I remembered the rush of power that I felt when she touched me. I could tell she didn't feel it with the same intensity I had. Could it be that she has no idea what or who she is?

Why did I, of all people, have to be the first one to meet her? I know for sure the others would have said something if they'd stumbled across her first. They believed in the fairy tale we've been fed all these years. Damn it, why is my power reacting like this? I didn't spend the last five years learning to manage it for one woman to ruin it.

I thought back to the archive room. I'd felt my power flare and reach out towards something it was drawn to. I assumed it was sensing one of the lesser demons that we've been hunting nearby, so I ignored it. It wasn't until seconds before she sat on me that I knew someone was in the room with me. No one other than the Elementi used this obscure records room, and students needed permission from one of the Elementi to get access. So, imagine my surprise when the fragrance of rose wafted into my nose. The aroma was light and delicate, pure almost. I took another deep breath, and this time, the scent was stronger as if the source had gotten closer to me. That's when it crashed onto my chest, knocking the air and the crap out of me.

I shook my head, trying to get the memory of her crystal-blue eyes looking at me out of my head. I knew it was futile, I would be dreaming about those eyes for days. Even just thinking about her, I could still feel the current of power flowing between us as if she were still here. I had to fight the urge to go back and talk to her again, just to see if I'd dreamed the whole thing up.

What the hell is happening to me?

"Damn, Micah! Larry is going to be pissed that you damaged a four-hundred-year-old building. What's up?" Brayden asked, pulling me out of my thoughts.

I looked up to see my best friend leaning against the wall in front of me. He must've seen me punching the wall – a common occurrence for me when I was royally pissed.

"I think I might have just met the infamous sixth element," I said, brushing the stone chips from my bleeding knuckles.

Brayden's brows shot up and his eyes widened with surprise. He pushed away from the wall and walked over to me. "What makes you say that?"

"A strange girl was in the special archive and managed to sit on me," I said, wrapping the cloth hankie Brayden always kept on him around my bleeding hand.

"As entertaining as it is to hear that it happened to you of all people, I can't say that would be enough to qualify her as Synergy," Brayden teased.

My parents died when I was twelve, and I moved in with the Doltens. Our families had always been close, so it worked out for the best. I was an only child, and my extended family wasn't really interested in raising a kid that wasn't their own. Brayden's family was so welcoming to me. So, believe it when I say that Brayden knew just how much I didn't care for social interaction and took great joy in this happening to me.

"Har, har, har' Let's poke fun at the antisocial orphan. Nice move, asshole," I said with mock anger.

Brayden shrugged his shoulders. "So, I'm assuming something else happened for you to think this person could be Synergy."

"I can't explain it, but when her body made contact with mine, it was like I was sixteen again, and my powers just manifested. It was wild, out of control. It was all I could do to keep from setting the room on fire," I said, trying to explain the experience.

Brayden, who seemed to finally be taking me seriously, tapped his index finger on his chin. He always did that when his brain worked overtime figuring out a problem. "Out of all five of us, you have the greatest control over your powers, so for you to have that ripped away from you is something significant to consider."

"Why don't you ponder the universe later with Hudson? We have demons to kill. The sun has finally set, and I want to find them before they end up on the campus grounds," I said, walking toward the parking lot where my car was waiting.

"What section did Beth give us tonight?" Brayden asked, walking alongside me.

I pulled out my phone to double-check the text I'd gotten earlier. "Looks like the pasture lands between Aiden House and Ashfall Hall. Christ, that's a huge area! What does she think we are?"

"Magically-gifted descendants of the Knights Templar," Brayden deadpanned.

"Looks who's a funny man tonight," I said, frowning at him. I mumbled under my breath, "Dick."

We walked up to my bright, fire-engine red Bugatti Veyron and slid into the low sports car.

"Remind me again why we can't take my car? It's much less conspicuous than this," Brayden said, giving me a reproachful look.

"Because I'm not riding in that futuristic egg you call a car. I don't care if BMW made it; I'm still not going to ride in it," I said, pushing the button and letting the engine roar to life.

"At least mine isn't killing the earth one hit of a button at a time," Brayden grumbled.

"If you start on that bullshit with me again, I'm going to kick you out of my car, best friend or not. I let you talk me into a reusable straw and a bamboo toothbrush, but do not diss my car while you're in it," I snapped as I slammed down on the gas pedal, letting the rear wheels smoke before we launched forward.

Brayden opened his mouth, his face showing his disapproval on my burn out. "Not a word, Brayden."

He made the smart choice and kept his thoughts to himself as we drove the access road to the pastures. The night was clear, and the moon was bright, so it would be easy to wander through the fields looking for demons.

The world has no idea about the hidden battle that's been raging for almost a thousand years. Demons and angels have been fighting since the dawn of time, but it wasn't until the demons decided to try a different tactic that they started to involve us—the blessed Elementi. There are many levels of demons, and typically, the school was warded by the five blessed Elementi warriors. Over the past seven hundred years, those blessed Elementi have helped to keep the demons from taking over, but the demons were getting smarter and stronger. Meanwhile, the Elementi were stuck with the first generation of blessed Elementi who couldn't all be in the same room together without fighting. With this fatal flaw, lesser demons were finding their way through the cracks, and they were all heading in the same direction: the school.

I parked the car at the end of the access road. Brayden and I got out and started our search grid. Every night we paired up into two groups of two, rotating who we worked with, keeping the school safe. I was thankful that I had Brayden tonight, Beth had taken it as her mission to get Parker and me to get along by forcing us to patrol together. Thankfully, he had the night off and was stuck doing homework.

"Micah!"

I spun on my heel and ran after Brayden as he chased after something. I channeled my powers, producing my blessed weapons—two black swords, slightly curved with leather-wrapped handles—formed in my hands in a swirl of red energy. Ahead, I saw a burst of green coming from Brayden, and he pulled up the earth around the demon, trapping it in on all sides.

I charged past him and leaped over the wall of dirt, landing in front of the little demon. Thankfully this one didn't have wings, but I saw Brayden raise the walls around it just in case, blocking us from view. It snarled at me, its tiny mouth full of needle-sharp teeth that wanted nothing more than to tear me apart. This one was the size of a two-year-old and had claws for hands that whipped out at me, catching me across the side of my arm.

"Okay, asshole, you want to play dirty? I can play dirty," I said, absorbing my swords and replacing them with two balls of flickering flames. I chucked one after the other at its feet, causing it to jump to avoid them. "Take that, ya little fucker."

"Micah, cut that shit out and get it over with. We have more ground to cover," Brayden hollered from the other side of the wall.

Knowing Brayden was right, I produced my swords again and charged at the distracted demon. Crisscrossing my swords, I sliced its head off in one motion and blood spurted out. The moment it hit the ground, it drifted away, sizzling into smoke.

"All clear," I called out so Brayden knew he could drop the wall.

The dirt around me crumbled back to the earth, letting me go free. Brayden, with his arms crossed, glowered at me. "How many times has Liam told you to just get in, get it done, and get out? We need to make sure we don't get discovered."

"The Elementi have been undiscovered for almost eight hundred years, I don't think taking my time killing a demon will crash our hidden empire," I said, dusting the demon blood residue from my pants.

"Did the demon get you?" Brayden asked, noticing the tears in my sleeve.

"It's just a scratch," I said, waving it off.

Ignoring me, he hit his speed dial and lifted the phone to his ear. "You know that demons carry venom in their claws, who's to say you won't drop dead in an hour?" Brayden said as he waited for whoever to pick up the phone. "Professor Creed, it's Brayden. Micah got scratched by a lesser demon. Do we need to have him come in?"

Brayden paused to listen to the answer, he gave Creepy Creedy the description of the demon, said yes and no a few times, then hung up. "Looks like you'll live, it was a scouting demon, not a lethal one."

"So, you're telling me I'm gonna live," I said, rolling my eyes in mock relief. "Looks like you're stuck with me for a while longer."

"Shut up, come on, we still have a lot of ground to cover," Brayden said, walking past me and punching me in my unwounded shoulder.

The rest of our patrol was uneventful, and when it reached midnight we decided to head back. I never picked early classes, but Brayden was one of those strange early-bird-who-gets-the-worm guys, so he had a class at seven. Before we left, I popped the trunk and pulled out the first aid kit to wrap my arm so I wouldn't get any blood on my leather seats. Brayden helped me tie it off, tired of watching me struggle with it.

"Hey, did that chick ever text you?" I asked once we got back in the car and headed back to school.

"No, but I've seen her in passing at school. It looks like she's in deep with her studies. Always has her nose in a book," Brayden said, shrugging his shoulders.

Out of the five of us, Brayden and Parker had the biggest following of girls, but I was surprised to find out just how many fans Hudson had. With the way Jay avoided attention, I'm not sure that anyone knew he was even attending classes at school. I tried to follow in his footsteps, but somehow, I also managed to have a fan group. I tried everything in my power to ignore them, but they still left notes and things for me in my mailbox. That's why I had to resort to hiding out in the special archives room if I wanted to be left alone on the main campus.

"Maybe she's more of an in-person girl, she could be like you and suck at technology." I grinned, looking over at him.

"I can manage a phone just fine. It's when it comes to computers that I have a problem. When I run into problems, I just have our resident tech mogul fix it for me," Brayden said.

"At least Parker's good for one thing," I said, pulling into my parking spot in the teacher parking area.

"Not all of us can own a country and have family ties with powerful political figures," Brayden countered, smirking at me.

"Whatever. It's not like I've even been to the country I own. My extended family won't let me have access to any of my inheritance, except the money. Once I turn twenty-one, everything will finally be made available for me to look over," I said, irritated with the fight that my aunt and I had before school started.

"Hey man, I didn't mean to hit a sore subject," Brayden said, gripping my shoulder in an apology.

"It's fine, I didn't tell you about the fight with Aunt Muriel," I said, shaking him off and slapping him on the back, letting him know we were good.

Out of the corner of my eye, I saw what looked like a naked child run around the corner of a building. "You've got to be fucking kidding me. What have Jay and Hudson been doing all night?"

I took off in the direction that I'd seen the little demon disappear, knowing Brayden would follow. The little bastard was fast as it zigzagged around buildings, sticking to the shadows. Just when I thought I'd caught up to it, I lost sight of it. When it reappeared, it was running across the road toward Ashfall Hall.

"Brayden—the dorm!" I called as I shot off after it.

Brayden tried to box it in, but the demon sprouted wings and flew. We couldn't do anything too noticeable right in front of the biggest dorm, that had floor-to-ceiling windows. The demon flew the rest of the way to the dorm with us tracking its every move. It managed to find a small open window in what I guessed was a bathroom.

"We need to get inside; looks like it's on the third floor. Do you know if that was the girls' side, or the guys'?" Brayden asked as he swiped his keycard through the reader, unlocking the door.

"How would I know? That would be something Parker would know; I never visit the dorms," I snapped, yanking the door open and jogging over to the stairs on the right-hand side.

This was the one time I would ever thank Liam for making us train on the stair machine all the time. I took the steps two at a time until we made it to the third floor.

"Let's spread out, you go right, I'll go left. Text once one of us kills the little shit," I whispered harshly, short of breath.

Brayden nodded and took off. I walked quickly down to the end of the hall, where I found the bathroom. I was hoping that it was still trapped in there and couldn't manage the door latch. I turned the knob slowly until I heard screaming. Girls burst out of the bathroom, knocking me out of the way. *Guess it's the girls' side.* I waited till the stampede of girls passed, and then I ducked through the door. The demon was fighting off a wet towel that someone had apparently thrown at it. It tried to dart past me, but I tossed a fireball without thinking and watched as it hit the towel, bursting it into flames and causing the fire alarm to go off. The high-pitched blaring of the alarm threw the demon off, causing it to freeze in its tracks, and giving me the chance to run my sword through it. Wiping the water out of my face, I looked around the bathroom at all the sprinklers going off.

"Beth is going to skin me alive for this," I muttered as I trudged my way out of the bathroom. My clothes were soaked through. Thankfully, the rest of the building didn't have the sprinklers on, but all the girls were emerging bleary-eyed from their rooms to evacuate the building.

I found Brayden waiting for me in the lobby, and we walked out together into the crowd of sleepy students. We tried to weave our way through the mass to head back to Aiden House, when I crashed right into a blonde-haired, blue-eyed, rose-scented woman.

Fuck my life.

Lailah

"You have got to be fucking kidding me! Do you need glasses or something? Or are you just that much of a klutz?" a voice I distinctly remember from earlier that night said.

I looked up, greeted once again by those disdainful blue eyes, but this time he was soaking wet. Brayden appeared beside him, shocking me even more. How could someone so kind be friends with this asshat?

"Micah," Brayden said, smacking him on the backside of his head. "What the hell, man?"

The guy I now knew as Micah rubbed the back of his head and scowled at Brayden.

"I'm so sorry, Lailah, I don't know what comes over him. When he's in public, he forgets how to act like a human," Brayden said, trying to manage his friend's blunder.

"Why are you wet?" I asked, still not able to get past that fact.

"Matters that don't concern you," Micah grumbled. "Come on, Brayden. We need to get back."

"I hate to do this to you again, but I do have to go," Brayden apologized. He turned to go but then paused and looked back at me. "I hope you decide to reach out sometime soon. I would love a chance to really sit down and talk with you."

"I'll see where I can fit you into my schedule; I promise," I said as he walked off after Micah.

"What were Micah and Brayden doing here?" Cami asked as she walked up behind me.

I looked over my shoulder at her. "I have no idea. Wait, is Micah one of The Manor guys, too?"

"Yeah, he's Brayden's best friend. They grew up together, they're like brothers," Cami explained.

"The building is clear, you can all go back inside," someone shouted from the front of the building.

"How was your family dinner?" I asked as we walked back into the dorm. Cami shrugged. "Everything okay?" It was unlike her to be so quiet about things—good or bad.

"It's fine, Lala. Things are just changing faster than I'd like," Cami said cryptically as we got on the elevator.

"What does that mean? Do you think I'm going to abandon you for some guy? Is that what this is about? I haven't even texted Brayden since he gave me his number," I said, making sure that Cami knew she was number one in my life.

"You haven't texted him?! Lala, do you know what a bitchy thing that is to do to a guy?" Cami said, pulling me out of the elevator on her floor. "You like him, right?"

I paused to think about that; I did like Brayden a lot, but I could also say that I had a thing for Parker too after the party.

"Yes, but he's not the only one I think I like," I said, deciding to be honest with her and myself.

Cami raised her brows at this announcement. "Oh, well, I guess that does make things more interesting. Still, you're not dating anyone, so there's no harm in trying out a few different guys before settling on one, or both."

"Both!" I said, shocked. She opened the door to her room, holding it open for me to follow. "Why would I pick both? There is no way I could handle seeing two guys separately. Also, that's a dick move to make. Way worse than not texting them at all."

"Lala, honey, this is twenty-twenty; if you want two boyfriends, who's to say you can't?" Cami challenged. "Hell, I could have a girlfriend and a boyfriend if I ever cared to."

I laughed at the excitement on her face at the idea. "I couldn't even make a relationship work with one guy, how could I manage to keep two guys happy?"

"See, that's where you're wrong," Cami said, waving a finger at me. "It's not your job alone to make anyone happy in any relationship, ours included. They take effort from both sides. If you're the only one paddling the boat, then you're just going in circles. You need your partner—or partners—to put in the same, if not more, effort."

"Where were you four years ago when I needed to hear that?" I asked, sitting on the edge of her bed, which was the only clean surface in the room.

"You have to go through the bad to understand how good the right thing is," Cami said, flopping onto her bed behind me. "Let's have a sleepover since you're already here, it's one a.m., tomorrow is Tuesday, and we both have late starts. It's perfect."

I shrugged, looking around the room and seeing how every surface was covered in clothes, accessories, and food wrappers. "Um, I don't see anywhere for me to sleep. I think there might be a couch under that mountain of clothes."

"Sleep next to me, the bed's big enough, and I promise not to turn you into a lesbian after a night with me," Cami teased.

I laughed, shaking my head at her. "I wasn't worried about that; who's to say I won't take advantage of you and add you to my growing list."

"Don't tease me with things that will never happen, Lala, it's just cruel," Cami said, wriggling under the blankets and making room for me.

"Sweet dreams then, it's the only place that would be able to happen," I said with a giggle, glad to finally dish back some of the sass I always got.

The next morning, I woke with Cami wrapped around me like an anaconda. I had to pee so bad, but any time I moved, she would hold tighter. Finally, when I'd tried to wake her up nicely—and failed, I decided I needed to resort to desperate measures. I readied myself, knowing it was going to hurt, then rolled off the edge of the bed and landed on the floor.

"Fuck, I'm up, what happened?" Cami said, popping up from the floor, ready for anything.

I started to laugh as she turned from side to side, looking for whatever caused us to fall out of the bed. "Serves you right, I needed to pee," I said, picking myself up off the floor and heading out of the room.

"Not cool, Lala, see if I ever invite you for another sleepover!" she yelled as I left.

I took the elevator up to my own room and grabbed things I would need to shower and get ready for the day. When I glanced at my clock, I was surprised to see it was only eight-thirty. I had plenty of time this morning, since my first class didn't start until eleven. I couldn't be late. It was a hands-on lab class for chemistry that I needed to do well in. I headed down the hall to shower, passing by a bunch of girls who were putting on their makeup at the large mirror over the sinks. As I walked by, their chatter died out, and they watched me with stony silence. I ignored them and set my clothes on the bench outside the shower so they wouldn't get wet. I grabbed my towel and shower things and stepped into the first open stall. I took my time letting the hot water run over my skin, enjoying the luxury of not being in a hurry for once. I even took the time to shave my legs while I let a deep conditioner sit in my hair.

Finished, I wrapped up in my towel and walked out to find my clothes were missing. The only thing left in their place was a Post-it with *leave The Manor boys alone or else* written on it in angry block letters. How charming. I crumpled the note up, glad that I brought my towel in with me or else I would've been left with nothing. The calm that I felt in the shower was thrown to the wayside as I stormed down the hall back to my room. When I got there, I realized that one of the things they took was my Notre Dame sweatshirt. I threw on some clothes and ran around the dorm, trying to find where they put my clothes. I finally went around the back of the dorm to where the dumpster was and opened the lid. Sure enough, they had thrown all my clothes away.

How dare those fucking bitches do this? What the hell had I ever done to them? I didn't ask for The Manor boys to decide to talk to me. I would love it if they stopped talking to me after this. I paused at that thought. *Did I really want to let some insecure bitches control what I did or who I talked to? Nope. Now I wanted to spend all my time with those guys just to piss them off. I think I'll go text Brayden right now.*

Heading back to my room, I tossed the clothes into my dirty basket so I could wash them later. I grabbed my phone and scrolled down to Brayden's number. Riding on the high of my anger, I typed out a simple message asking him when he would be free. Then I decided I was way too worked up to get anything done. I needed to do something to relieve all this stress that school had built up in me. I thought back to the last time I'd gone for a run and realized it had been almost three weeks. That was part of my problem, I always found I handled life better when I ran.

I switched into running clothes, selecting my favorite tank top that said, "I'm a ray of fucking sunshine." I piled my still-wet hair on top of my head and slipped my room key into the pocket of my shorts, zipping it closed. The last thing I needed was to get locked out of my room. I looked at my phone and decided against taking it with me. I just wanted to be left alone. I looked over the school map that I had from orientation and saw that there was a path running around the school property. It looked like an easy three miles and hard for me to get lost on.

I decided to go down the stairs to get my blood pumping and ready me for my run. When I reached the bottom, I stretched out my legs a little, so I wouldn't get a cramp along the way and headed off. Once on the asphalt path, I zoned out, letting the sound of my breathing and the slapping of my shoes on the ground be the only things I focused on. The pure joy of running filled me like a long-lost friend. I needed to make this a routine again, it would keep me from losing my shit while stuck in a building of evil women.

As I ran, I felt my legs getting tired, my breathing becoming more labored, and my pulse rose slightly. *That's strange, I can run three miles easily, it's when I get closer to six that I start getting winded. Am I that out of shape?* I stopped and took a moment to catch my breath, shaking out my legs. I looked around and froze—I was nowhere near the school. I didn't even have my watch on to know what time it was. *How long have I been running?*

I turned around and started walking back the way I came, giving my legs a chance to recover. I didn't know how long it would take me to get back. I kept looking around to find a glimpse of the school trying to get a read on what direction to head. I felt my panic begin to rise as I kicked myself for leaving without my phone. What kind of an idiot am I? Feeling the need to move faster, I started jogging again, hoping I might run into someone on the path.

As if the gods had heard me, a half-naked guy came running up behind me and passed me with long powerful steps. His golden skin was glistening with sweat, drawing my eyes to watch him as he ran, making me forget I needed help.

"Hey!" I yelled, waving at him to get his attention.

He slowed, then stopped looking back at me with a blank expression, his chest heaving as he caught his breath. *Don't just drool over him, ask him for help, you idiot*, I chided myself.

"Sorry to stop you on your run, but I seem to have taken a wrong turn," I said and waited for some response.

He just silently looked at me with his gorgeous almond-shaped eyes that were the color of slate. He blinked slowly at me and ran his hand over his buzzed head. It was then I noticed the tattoos covering his whole left arm in a black and white design that went over his shoulder and dipped onto his pec. Finally, he nodded at me and started jogging again slightly slower.

I looked around to see if there was anyone else who could help me or if I would have to manage with the silent Asian god. *Who am I kidding? Why wouldn't I follow the half-naked man?* I took off, jogging to catch up with him. Now that I felt more rested and I had a guide to keep me from freaking out, I picked up my normal pace. I fell back into my zone and smiled at the sound of both of us matching paces. Part of me wanted to push my stride longer to see if I could keep up with his original pace. I knew better than to do that this far into the run, and I didn't know how long I was going to need to last.

In our companionable silence, I took the time to appreciate having a running partner for once. I used to be on the track team in high school and never minded being a lone runner. I think it happened because I didn't have anyone who could match my stride, let alone push me further. Even though I was only five-three and didn't have the typical legs for running, I made up for it in speed and stamina. At my peak performance, when I added hurdles to the list, I could run a half marathon for a warm-up. I was shaken out of my reminiscing when a hand grabbed my arm and pulled me to the right.

"This way, if you want to head back to school," a rich deep voice said beside me.

I looked up, shocked to hear him speak for the first time. "Thanks. I would've been running to another country if you hadn't been here," I said, grinning.

"No, you would have ended up running all the way to Nettleton, which is another twenty-four clicks from here," he said.

Okay, this guy doesn't do sarcasm well apparently, but since he's willing to talk, why not take advantage.

"How far did I manage to run off course?" I asked, slowing a little to make talking easier.

"Close to fifteen clicks give or take," he said, matching my pace.

"Clicks?" I asked confused. I'd only heard military people use this term.

I saw the corner of his mouth pull up like he might smile. "It's nine point three miles."

"Holy crap! How did I manage to get that off track?" I said more to myself than him.

"By the time we make it back, I would say it will be around seventeen total. I'm taking you back a more direct route to the school," he explained.

"Oh, God. I'm going to be so sore tomorrow. It has been way too long for me to run that far," I complained.

My running partner shrugged his shoulders. "I think the body can handle more than we give it credit for. You're an experienced runner, you'll be fine."

"How can you tell that?" I asked, intrigued.

"You lose yourself in your running. Only people who have been running for a while know how to tune out everything but the run," he said, looking at me out of the corner of his eye. "Also, not many people can get close to matching my preferred pace."

I grinned widely. I didn't know why, but I felt like it was something he didn't often do. When I looked down the path rounding a shrub wall, I saw the school dead ahead. *I wasn't lost forever!* I picked up my pace looking over to my right, where I found him watching me with the first glimmer of emotion in his eyes. He saw my challenge for what it was. He edged past me, pushing the pace faster. I rose to the bait and nosed past him. Soon we were both running full tilt down the path, not a care in the world. My bun jostled loose from its confines, and I saw my scrunchie fall to the ground. I didn't care; I had a race to win and an ass to beat.

I gritted my teeth as I felt my energy begin to waver, I couldn't let up yet. The school was so close it was only a few more feet that I had to make, and I would be waiting for him to brush off my dust. Just when I thought I had this in the bag, I saw him blur past me; he'd been holding back till the very end. I knew I'd been beat. I didn't have anything left in the tank, so I slowed to a more manageable pace. Once I caught up to him near the reflecting pool where I'd started this run, I flopped into the grass.

"You run like the flippin' wind. Where did you have that last boost stored away?" I asked, looking up at him from the ground.

I was happy to see that he had to take a moment to catch his breath before answering. "It's always the best tactic to let your foe think they've won. It makes them careless."

I blinked up at him, surprised by that nugget of information. "You read the *Art of War* before bed, don't you."

"It might be a personal favorite, but no, I didn't learn that from there," he said, reaching a hand to help me up. "You shouldn't let your legs freeze up like that or you will be sore tomorrow."

As he helped me up, I looked down at his watch and gasped. "Oh, fuck!"

He looked at me questioningly, looking down at his watch. "Is there something about the time being noon that offends you?"

"No, it's not that. I can't believe I was gone that long. I left for my run at nine-thirty; it was supposed to take me forty-five minutes at most to do this run. It's now been over three hours, and I totally missed my lab for a class I can't screw up in," I said, sitting dejectedly on the low brick wall of the reflecting pool. "Why did I choose Organic Chemistry of all things?"

My savior came and sat next to me, rigid and unsure. "I'm sorry you missed an important class."

"It wouldn't be so bad if I wasn't already sucking at it. The other day it took me an hour to do a simple twenty-question quiz. I'm going to bomb this class and lose my scholarship if I can't perform to the school standards," I said, wallowing in my self-pity.

"Would it help if I knew of someone who could tutor you?" he asked, tilting his head to the side.

"That would be amazing, but I don't really have the extra money to pay someone."

"He wouldn't charge you. He has no need for the extra income."

"Sure, sounds like a dream come true," I said, smiling up at him.

He pulled his cell phone from his pocket and handed it to me. "Put your number in, and I'll text you his number. He'll be glad to help if you tell him Jay gave you his number."

I smirked at him as I typed in my number, "Is that your name—Jay?"

"It's Jalen, but everyone calls me Jay," he answered as I handed him back his phone.

"You'll find my name under Lailah, but since you only have ten contacts, I'm sure you would have figured it out," I said, standing up.

"I hate phones, but it's how everyone chooses to communicate these days," Jay said, following my lead. "Let me know if you want a guide on your next run. I know all the trails around here."

"Thanks, I think I'll take you up on that offer," I said, waving goodbye as I crossed the street to Ashfall.

Eleven

Jay

I watched as Lailah made it across the street to her dorm, waiting to make sure she didn't get lost again. I looked down at my phone, which now had her number in it. *Why did I feel the need to help her? Normally, I wouldn't have stopped to help someone on the trails. If they got lost, they could figure out how to get back, it would be a valuable lesson.*

When she called out to me, I felt a tug demanding me to stop and see what was going on. When I looked back to see this small woman with desperate crystal-blue eyes, I couldn't help but hear what she needed. I quickly typed out Hudson's number and sent it to her, then sent another one letting her know it was coming from me. Tucking my phone back in my pocket, I turned and headed off to Aiden House. I had a meeting that I needed to get ready for with my father. There was a new company that was looking to use our private security company.

Even though I was part of the Elementi Warriors, my father still had me working alongside him. He was loyal to the Elementi cause, but saw our group of warriors as a hindrance to the mission. We'd been training together during the summers since some of us were about fifteen. Now that we were in college, and at Ryevick to get our education and more intensive training as a team, we were failing. My father worked with Liam from time to time, improved our methods, and witnessed our failure at restoring the wards.

Deciding my skills would be better used in his company, I had limited classes at school; in fact, I only had the one required for the Elementi. I wasn't really bothered by it; I prefer not to be forced to interact with the typical student body. It was chaotic, messy, and loud. One couldn't think clearly in all that busyness. I much preferred doing my studies in the mansion where I could have the private library all to myself. Hudson would join me there, but we both liked the pure silence, so it worked.

As for the others, having to live with Brayden and Micah wasn't too much of a hassle, they kept to themselves. Parker was the problem in the group; he didn't take anything seriously. He was forever playing practical jokes on everyone. He tried to do that to me once, but when he woke up with fire ants in his bed the next day, he decided never to do it again. Wise choice on his part. I wanted our team to be successful, but I refused to put in the effort when none of the others did either. They all had other goals they wanted to achieve that had nothing to do with being an Elementi Warrior.

My phone vibrated in my pocket. It was a response from Lailah.

Lailah: **Thanks for the help today and the number! Oh, I plan to run every morning at 6am to get back into my running routine if you want to join me**

I couldn't help but smirk, liking the thought of having her as my running buddy.

Me: Tomorrow, reflecting pool, 0600.

Twelve

Lailah

When I made it back to the dorm, I checked my phone and, sure enough, Jay had texted me the number. I laughed at how direct he was in his messages. I'd also gotten a response from Brayden on when he would be available to meet up. I decided to get back to him after I took another shower, taking my clothes with me for safekeeping. I hurried out of the dorm and off to English class, trying not to miss my only other class for the day.

Thankfully, English was one class that I didn't have to worry too much about. I was good at writing, and this one was a basic class that all students had to take. Heading to the coffee shop, I got my beloved chai and decided to reach out to this guy Jay suggested.

Me: Hello, you don't know me but your friend Jay gave me your number. I am

> **struggling in organic chem and he said you might be able to help me.**

Here's to hoping he would reply. I pulled out my schedule and looked over what projects I had coming up and what tests I would need to be prepared for. Feeling like I could step back the next week and do something fun, I texted Brayden back, feeling kind of nervous.

> Me: **Hey, so Thursday works for me if you want to meet up at the coffee shop.**

I pulled out my notes from what I had found in the special archives and started picking out what I could use for my paper. I was so focused on my work that when my phone vibrated loudly on the table, I jumped. I glanced at it and saw that it was a response from the mystery tutor.

> Mystery Tutor: **Jay gave you my number? How do you know him?**

> Me: **Bit of a strange story, but he rescued me when I got lost on a run. As we were talking, I told him about not doing so hot in my class, and he said you would help me. I hope I didn't overstep in reaching out to you.**

I knew I shouldn't have trusted a guy I'd just met and a strange phone number. This is how people get catfished and crap like that. This guy must have thought I was an idiot for believing this rando running around school grounds.

Mystery Tutor: **No, it's fine. Just surprised. Jay doesn't mingle much. I am free tomorrow after 4pm if that works for you. We can meet at one of the study labs in the library.**

I breathed a sigh of relief; this guy wasn't a joke.

Me: **I can make that work, thank you for doing this!**

Mystery Tutor: **Sure thing, I'll text you the study room number tomorrow.**

"Thank God," I said, dropping my head on my notebook in relief.

"What's up with you, Lala? Did you have someone roll you off the bed at an ungodly early hour because they needed to pee? Oh, wait, no, that was me," Cami said, plunking her stuff down across from me.

"Hey, if you hadn't wrapped yourself around me, I wouldn't have had to do that. I tried to wake you up before jumping to such drastic measures," I said in my defense.

Cami rolled her eyes and took a long pull on her monster-sized coffee. "Whatever, how has your day been? I haven't seen you at all."

"It's been a day, let me tell you. First, I got my clothes stolen and tossed in the dumpster. Then, I went on a run to clear my head and got lost running almost twenty miles. Thank God someone happened to be running in the same area, and he helped me get back. If that all wasn't enough, because I got lost, I missed a lab class for Organic Chem. Those are big deals, Cami," I said, exasperated at the whole day.

Cami sat back in her chair and looked me up and down. "You can run twenty miles and still look this good, damn I'm impressed."

"Out of all that, running twenty miles is what you zeroed in on?" I asked, shaking my head.

"What? It's impressive," she said in her defense.

I shrugged my shoulders, "It's not really. I used to run twenty miles on a normal basis and did marathons for fun when it was off-season."

"Kill me now!" Cami said, shivering at the thought. "I would never run like that for fun, sounds more like torture."

I laughed and took a swig from my now-cold chai. "Oh! I meant to tell you this earlier, but the day got away from me. So, when I went to the special archives yesterday, I took the chance to do some investigating into the Elementi."

Cami stilled and peered at me over her coffee cup. "What did you find?"

I leaned in, excited to share. "So, it looks like the first mention of it is when the Knights Templar had this huge battle and lost, it was toward the end of the golden era of the Knights. After the battle, they splintered off and started being known as the Elementi."

"So, are they rogue knights?" Cami asked, frowning.

I shook my head, waving off her comment. "No, they went off to help defend many small towns and villages that became super prominent places later on. It's like anywhere they went, some influential person popped up from there sometime later. If they'd gotten wiped out, then we wouldn't have some of the most brilliant minds in the world."

"How crazy is that? Do you think they might have known these places were going to be important or could it just be chance?" Cami asked, setting down her coffee.

I grinned, knowing I had her full attention now. "I don't have a clue, but don't you think it's crazy that they always seemed to be around when something important was going down? When I dug a little deeper about the places where they were spotted, strange occurrences happened afterward at each one."

"Strange occurrences?" Cami asked.

"Yeah, like a massive rainstorm, earthquake, forest fire, or tornado. There was even a mention about people having mass hallucinations, and a whole town believed angels came down from heaven and possessed them," I said, letting that hang for Cami to mull over.

"Why would angels possess people?" Cami ventured.

"According to my research, these people were saved because they all were woken up and walked out of town before a volcano erupted. It would have been Pompeii all over again. When the village woke up, they were all in boats out on the sea, safe and sound." I flipped through my notebook to see what else I had discovered.

"Are you saying you think this Elementi splinter group is causing all these strange things?" Cami questioned, scrunching up her face.

Leaning back in my chair, I sighed and stared up at the ceiling of the coffee shop. "It's crazy, right? This is the real world, not some fantasy story where the impossible can happen." I looked back at Cami and gave a wistful smile. "I guess I'm connecting things that probably have nothing to do with each other."

"You never know, Lala, maybe it would take someone who believed in the impossible to see the truth," Cami said with a look in her eyes that I couldn't place.

"You might be right, but I have lots of other things to study that are more important than that. It's my first semester, and I'm already on the way to failing a class," I said, closing my notebook and the topic.

"You're done with classes, right? We should go into town since you've had such a crappy day. You can get those sugar cookies you love so much," Cami said, wagging her eyebrows, knowing that was the one thing I couldn't say no to.

"Sounds like fun," a male voice said behind us.

The look on Cami's face was enough to tell me it had to be Parker. I knew that they got along better than they liked to let on, but I'd figured it out. I tilted my head back, and sure enough, Parker was right behind me with his signature grin.

"Who said you're invited, dickweed?" Cami shot at him.

He pulled over a chair and sat on it backward as he leveled his gaze to Cami. "Lailah is my friend, too. You can't keep her to yourself all the time. Sharing is caring, Camilla, I know Beth taught you better than that."

Cami's hand shot out, and she had Parker's hand with his thumb twisted at an awkward angle, and his face twisted in pain. "Call me that one more time. Go on, I dare you," Cami growled.

"Uncle, uncle I give, I give," Parker said, trying to twist his body to lessen the pain.

Cami released him, tossing his hand away like it was going to bite her. "I better never hear that out of your mouth again, or I really will break off your thumb, ya douche-canoe."

"Wait! Is that what Cami is short for?" I asked. "I never would have guessed you as a Camil—"

"I love you, Lala, but if you finish that sentence, I will bitch-slap the shit out of you," Cami said, glaring at me and scaring me with how intense she was about it.

"Okay, I'll forget I ever heard it," I said, raising my hands in submission.

"Look what you've done, ya twat waffle; you made me scare Lala," Cami said, turning her anger back on Parker.

"Why don't you keep from getting your panties in a knot and calm down," Parker said, holding his own against Cami.

I looked between the two of them and started to giggle. Hearing me, they paused their stare-down to look at me in surprise. The way they were so similar just struck me as funny. I couldn't explain it, but I loved seeing them go toe to toe. Getting myself under control, I waved them off and gathered my stuff.

"Come on, let's head into town so I can get my sugar fix," I said.

"Wanna ride with me?" Parker asked, giving me puppy-dog eyes.

I looked over at Cami with a questioning eyebrow, and she just smirked at me. "Sure, sounds good."

"Awesome. I have my ride in the faculty parking lot, so we don't have to go far," Parker said, giving me an excited smile.

"Parker, if you do something stupid and get Lala hurt, I will kill you, raise you from the dead, and kill you again. You feel me?" Cami said, giving Parker a stern look.

"Chill, I won't let anything happen to her," Parker grumbled.

We all walked out of the coffee shop, and I waved at Cami as she split off to grab her car from the dorms. I followed Parker until we stopped in front of a bright-yellow motorcycle. I felt my panic level rise as I realized why Cami had been worried about my safety. I looked up at Parker to tell him I changed my mind, but he settled his hands on my shoulders and looked me in the eye.

"I know I come off as an impulsive child, but I promise I will make sure you're safe," Parker searched my face before he grabbed the spare helmet from the saddlebag on his bike. "I'm not sure all your hair will fit in here, but let's give it a shot."

I laughed, my fear about the situation calming down. I pulled my hair out of its bun and jammed the helmet on over my head. It took a little wiggling, but I managed to get it to fit snugly on my head. Parker helped me with the chin strap, and having him so close gave me butterflies in my stomach. I could feel his body heat and the subtle scent of his cologne that smells like warm spices.

"Perfect," Parker said, patting the top of my helmet to let me know he was done.

I struggled not to blush, and I dipped my head so he couldn't see my face as I looked at the bike. "What kind of motorcycle is this?" I asked, knowing I would have no idea, but it gave me something else to think about.

"It's a Harley Davidson Fat Boy, smooth ride, but still stylish, just like me," Parker said with a wink.

At that comment, I lost the battle with my flushing cheeks, and I knew from the heat coming off my face that I was as bright as a stop sign. I coughed, choking on my own spit at the suddenness of the teasing. I knew Parker and I were becoming friends, and I knew I kind of liked him, but I didn't know we were at the flirty stage yet.

"Shit, I'm sorry, Lailah. I didn't mean to make you uncomfortable. I don't know how to have a friend that's a girl. I always have girls around, but they only want one thing from me. I know you're not like that. I shouldn't have said that, it just popped out," Parker said, groaning and rubbing his face with his hands.

I didn't know how I felt about him seeing me as just a friend, but I knew for sure I was happy that he saw me differently than those vipers that had tossed my clothes in the dumpster.

Recovered from my coughing fit, I reached out and patted him on the arm. "It's all good, I tend to be super awkward around people, so I get it, it happens. Come on, at this point, Cami is halfway there with how she drives."

"Yeah, and she was worried about me getting you hurt. She's a psycho when she drives. Her and Micah, one of my other dorm mates, used to have drag races all the time; they're just nuts," Parker said as he straddled his bike and pulled on his helmet.

"Oh, so you've known Micah for a long time, too?" I asked, surprised, thinking they had only met at school.

"Yeah, all of us who live at Aiden House have known each other for a long time. Our parents all mingle in the same social circle," Parker said offhandedly. "Okay, climb on."

I gulped and threw my leg over the machine and settled in behind Parker. I tried to keep some space between us, but the way the seat was designed made me slide right up against him. Since I couldn't keep my lower body away from him, I tried to lean back, so my chest wasn't resting on his back.

"I'm going to assume this is your first time on a motorcycle." He grabbed my hands from where they were resting on my legs and wrapped them around his middle. "Hold on to me tight and follow my lead. Lean into the curves, flow with the road, and stay relaxed, that's all there is to it," Parker instructed.

I gave in and let myself lean against him, reminding me of us dancing at the party. It didn't feel strange then, and it didn't now either. In many ways, it felt like I was right where I belonged, safe, comfortable, and almost like I was home. It gave me a zing of excitement, but it also made me worry that I was reading into things that weren't really there. Obviously, Parker didn't see me as more than a friend, and I needed to keep it that way. Parker was growing on me, and I didn't want to mess up and lose out on the friendship we could have. Parker pulled out slowly, letting me get a feel for the bike, but once we were on the main road, he kicked it into high gear, and we raced down the open road.

The ride was exhilarating, and I could see why people liked to ride motorcycles. It made you feel like you were free. The wind across your face, the scents of the world around you, and the speed were all intoxicating. It was close to the feeling I had while running, only way faster. It also helped to have Parker's warm body to cut the chill of the ride. All too soon, we made it to town and found a place to park. Parker held the bike steady while I hopped off, and he followed shortly after.

"What took you so long?" Cami called as she walked over to us.

"You told me to keep her safe, I was doing just that, don't be an ass," Parker retorted, locking the helmets up. "Just because you can get around the world in twenty minutes doesn't mean it's right."

"Whatever," Cami said, brushing off Parker's answer. "Oh, we need to stop by the book store for my sister. She texted me on my way over here. You guys need anything else while we're here?"

"Nope. I'm just along for the ride," Parker said, grinning at us.

I shook my head and headed off in the direction of delicious smelling cookies. This was exactly what I needed after the shitty day I'd had. I wondered what the girls will do next when they see me and Parker hanging out today and then me with Brayden later in the week. I smiled to myself, glad that I wasn't going to let them rule who I made friends with.

"Where are we off to?" Parker asked.

"The bakery to get God's gift to the human world," I said, humming to myself.

"Um, what?" Parker said, walking backward in front of me so he could see my face.

I rolled my eyes at him, no one ever understood my strange love for all things sugar cookie. "Remember when we first met, and you smashed my cookie?"

"Yeah, I still feel bad about that," he answered.

"That was a small piece of heaven you shattered. Some girls have an obsession with clothes, shoes, or coffee, but for me, it's all about the sugar cookies," I said, smiling when I saw him understand.

"Wow! So, I'm lucky you're even still talking to me after I murdered your cookie?" Parker said, letting out a low whistle.

"No, you're lucky Lala is more forgiving than I am. I would've written you off for good," Cami piped up.

"Hey, I bought her a new one, I took responsibility for my actions," Parker defended himself.

"Guys, come on, it's over and done with. That happened weeks ago," I said, trying to end the squabbling as we arrived at the bakery.

I pulled open the door and listened to the little chime signaling our arrival. I wandered over to the cookie display and started to search for the treasured item. Cami and I had never come this late in the day, and I got to the area where they were normally displayed, but it was empty. I quickly looked back through the cases on either side, but there was not a single sugar cookie in sight.

"Well, hello, Lailah, good to see you," Anne said, coming out of the back, wiping her flour-covered hands on her apron. "You're here much later than usual."

Parker turned to look at me with raised eyebrows. "Come here often?"

"Anne, am I too late? I don't see any in the display case," I asked, even I could hear the desperation in my voice.

"Oh, don't worry, love. I always have a batch set aside in the back just for you." Anne gave me a warm smile before she grabbed a box to place the cookies in.

"You're a real MVP, Anne," Cami said. "I think after the day Lailah's had, she might have gone catatonic right here in your bakery."

"Oh, I'm sorry to hear that. I'll go get them right away," Anne tutted before she returned to the back room for the cookies.

"Damn, you must really love those cookies if you're on a first-name basis with the baker," Parker said, enjoying watching this whole thing going down.

"I guess so, things have been so stressful with school, that Cami or I popped in to get cookies a few times. Anne is just super sweet and reminds me a lot of my mom, so we bonded," I said as Anne walked back to us.

"I have never met someone who has such a mature palate when it comes to cookies. She can even tell me when I've added too much butter and not enough vanilla," Anne said, chuckling.

"My mom's also a baker, and I would taste test all her dough, so I learned from her. Other than Anne, I've never met someone who can make a better sugar cookie than my mom," I said proudly.

"Oh stop, you're going to make me blush," Anne said, waving a hand at us. "Now, those are on me tonight, love, seeing as you had a bad day and all."

"Bless you, Anne," I said, blowing her a kiss as we walked out the door.

Once out on the sidewalk, I couldn't help doing a little skip of happiness now that I was holding the magical white bakery box.

"So, is it off-limits to ask if you're willing to share?" Parker asked as we walked over to the bookstore.

I gave Parker a sideways glance, deciding how I was feeling about sharing my cookies with him. I liked Parker, but I felt like sharing my cookie wasn't a right he'd earned yet. A girl had to be careful who she gave her cookies to. You never knew if they would appreciate them the way they should be appreciated. I knew the value of that round golden sugary goodness, but would he treat it with the proper respect? That was yet to be determined.

"I'm not sure we've reached that level of friendship yet," I said and watched the shocked look on Parker's face.

"Seriously?" he complained.

"Look, cocknugget, *I* didn't even get my cookie until this week! Wait your turn," Cami said, wagging her eyebrows at him.

"Cami! Don't tell him that, you make it sound dirty," I shrieked.

"What? The way you treat your cookies, it might as well be sex," Cami said, nudging me with her elbow.

"Okay, I feel like this conversation has taken a turn that I am not comfortable with. My slight obsession with sugar cookies might be a little unorthodox, but it could be worse," I said, feeling my cheeks heat.

"Note to self: if I ever get you mad at me, I'll make sure to visit Anne right away," Parker said, laughing.

"What do you mean *if,* more like *when,*" Cami mumbled as she opened the door to the bookstore.

We walked in, and since I didn't really need anything, I decided to check out the fiction section. It was in the back of the bookstore next to the small music section where they sold old vinyl records and CDs. Parker trailed after me, seeming content to follow my lead. I headed to the fiction section and started pulling random books that caught my eye off the shelf. I picked up one book, and on the cover, the woman in the middle was surrounded by five half-naked men. I remember Cami telling me that dating more than one person wasn't as taboo as it used to be. Before I could turn it over to read the back of the cover, Parker reached over and plucked the book out of my hands. I looked over my shoulder at him as he looked over the book. He blinked a few times and then looked at me and back at the book.

"Is this the type of stuff you read?" he asked, his cheeks pinking up a little.

Was Parker embarrassed? Had the thought of sharing a woman with other guys made mister adventurous uncomfortable?

"No, but Cami keeps telling me I need to be more open-minded, so I figured why not," I teased, unable to let him shake off his embarrassment.

"You're saying that you'd be into being with more than one guy?" Parker asked.

I started to laugh at his reaction. How he thought I would ever have more than one guy interested in me was priceless. Also, as I said to Cami, I could barely manage one relationship, how could I deal with multiples?

"Parker, it's in the fiction section. That means it's for us women to dream about but doesn't actually happen in the real world, let alone for me," I answered, taking the book off his hands and putting it back on the shelf.

I headed out of the fiction section, thinking I might just need to come back for that book sometime. I looked over to my right and saw Micah flipping through the vinyl in the rock section. I ducked behind one of the lower bookshelves that made up the wall around the section. Parker looked down at me and then over at Micah. Seconds later, he was squatting next to me with a scowl on his face.

"Why are you hiding from Micah?" I whispered.

"Because he's a rat bastard, and I can't stand him," Parker answered in a loud attempt at a whisper.

"I can't say the few interactions we've had have been great, so I would rather avoid him," I said, trying to waddle by in my squatted position.

Just as we were about the clear the section, Micah walked by without sparing us a glance. "Parker, next time learn to whisper. We rats have good hearing."

Unable to hold it together, I landed on my ass, laughing hysterically. After all that had happened today, to end it being caught in such an awkward position was just too much to handle. Parker started cracking up next to me till we both had tears streaming down our cheeks.

"What the hell is wrong with you two idiots?" Cami asked us, her hands on her hips.

I shook my head, unable to answer her question. I tried to calm myself down by taking deep breaths, but I would just hear Micah's comment and lose it all over again. Truly this was what I really needed, friends, laughter, and cookies could fix anything.

Lailah

"Lailah, did the special archives help you with your paper?" Mr. Phillips asked as I handed him the first three pages of my paper.

"It was super helpful, but I have to say that I was shocked at the security. I've never seen a library have that kind of protected section before," I said.

"I imagine not, we are very blessed to have an archive of such old historical books. These are the only copies in the world, and we need to protect that history," Mr. Phillips explained.

"I couldn't agree more, it was so cool to read something that was written so long ago. Thank you very much for letting me have access," I said, smiling at him.

"My pleasure, it's students like you, who have such a thirst for history, which makes keeping that stuff around worth it. Now off you go, I don't want to hold you back from your next class," Mr. Phillips said, shooing me away from his desk.

I waved as I left the room and headed off for psych class. It was another riveting class going over our case study. I loved this class so much I almost wanted to change my major from history to psychology. I decided that I was going to take another class next semester and see if it was still as interesting when it wasn't the intro class. As I learned from Organic Chem, not everything was as interesting at the harder levels.

After having such a wonderful morning, I almost considered ditching my chem class. I knew we would be getting our quiz back, and I was not looking forward to seeing how badly I had done. We would also be moving on to a new topic, and I still didn't understand what we'd learned last week. I took my normal seat in the middle section and steeled myself to get my test back. Once everyone was in their seat, Professor Lark charged in with her TA close on her heels, holding a stack of papers.

"Well, class, I must say that these quizzes were atrocious. I think only two of you passed with a score of over seventy-five. I hope you take the feedback written on here by Hudson very seriously. It will be the only way to save yourself in this class," Professor Lark admonished, motioning for Hudson to pass out the tests.

Proceeding with the lesson, she turned her back on us and flipped to the first slide discussing acid-base reactions. Trying to follow along as best I could, I didn't notice right away that my test had been set next to me. I glanced over at it and felt the blood drain from my face. A large sixty-four written in red and circled glared up at me. I was so fucked if I couldn't get my act together. My tutoring session couldn't come soon enough. It was much too late to withdraw, and I needed to pass this class to keep my scholarship. I didn't care how it happened, but it needed to happen fast.

After class, I trudged my way to the coffee shop and ordered the biggest chai tea latte I could get. I even asked them to put whipped cream on it to make me feel better. I found my usual table and sat down to look over the test that I had bombed.

I read over the carefully written notes that the TA had left, and for the most part, I understood what I had done wrong. Tomorrow we have a lab, and because I missed one, I was behind on my practical application. I let my head fall onto my folded arms and groaned at the headache I could feel coming on.

"Someone looks like they need a cookie," Cami said as she slid into the seat across from me.

"I need more than a cookie to make this better," I grumbled. "Any chance you have something stronger hidden away in your room?"

"Lala, are you asking me if I have contraband in my dorm room? Would I go against school policy like that? I'm highly offended that you think that of me." Cami gasped.

I looked up from my spot on the table and frowned. "Right. And the water bottles in your mini fridge with the different colored caps are just so you know what day of the week to drink them."

"Drinking will not make Organic Chem any better. Don't you have your first tutoring session today?" Cami said, brushing off my snarkiness.

"Yeah, he's supposed to text me and let me know what room he set aside for us at four." I looked down at my watch. "I have two hours."

"Perfect. We can go get lunch, and I can try and get you out of this strange funk you're in," Cami said, grabbing my backpack and walking away. I quickly grabbed the rest of my things and headed after her.

Cami had me laughing halfway through lunch, forgetting how upset I was about my test. I looked down when my phone buzzed on the table and saw that my new tutor had texted me. I realized that I hadn't gotten the name of the guy I was going to be spending time with this evening. He gave me the study room number and confirmed that he would be there at four.

"Looks like I should head that way," I said to Cami.

"Lala, you have thirty minutes before you have to meet up. What's the rush?"

"You trust me to go to the library and find the study room in less time?"

"You've been doing so good lately, I figured this wouldn't be that bad." Cami shrugged.

"I'm not going to take any chances. With the test that I got back, there is no way I can mess this up. I'll text you when we finish," I said, picking up my tray and putting it on the belt that took it back to the kitchen.

I took a deep breath and headed over to the library. I had learned to navigate my normal routine just fine, but I didn't want to chance that I might get lost and miss the whole thing. Once I made it into the library, I walked up to the information desk.

"Hello, I'm looking for study room fifteen," I said, smiling at the woman behind the computer.

She peered over her screen, giving me a disapproving look. "Head up to the second floor, turn left, then head down the hall. It will be the room at the very end."

"Thanks."

For some reason, I felt like the lady was judging me, and I couldn't figure out why. I looked down at my shirt to make sure I didn't have anything spilled on it, then I realized what it said. I groaned. In big, bold letters, it said, *And then Satan said "Put the alphabet in math!"* I got this shirt from my older brother when I had a meltdown after failing my first math test. I guess it was fitting since this was the first time I was close to failing a class. Once up the stairs, I made my way down the hall as instructed. When I came to the last door, I didn't bother to knock, I just walked in. I looked up, hearing someone already in there.

"Sorry, I must have the wrong—" I halted when I saw Hudson, the TA from my chem class.

We both looked at each other for a moment, then he cleared his throat, standing up and reaching out his hand to me. "Lailah, right? Jay gave you my number for help with Organic Chem."

I felt my jaw drop at the realization of what was happening. Jay had given me the number of his friend who apparently was Hudson, which meant he was the last of the five who lived in The Manor. I then felt a blush creeping up my skin because I was going to be working with the one person, besides my teacher, who knew how badly I was doing in class. When I didn't take his hand, he pulled it back and used it to push his glasses back up his nose awkwardly.

"Sorry," I blurted, walking the rest of the way into the room. "Jay didn't actually tell me it was you whose number he gave me. I'm Lailah. It's nice to officially meet you." I held out my hand to him.

He grasped my hand in his firm, confident grasp, and gave it a solid shake. I felt a static shock between us, and I snatched my hand back from him. He gave me an apologetic smile and mumbled something sounding like sorry as he sat back down at the table between us. I took my seat and pulled out my books, notebook, and pen.

"The good part about this is that I already know what we've covered in class and what you're struggling with, so we can get right down to business," Hudson said, pulling out his own notes and textbook.

"Is there any hope for me? I never had trouble with science classes before, and I'm not sure why this one is causing me such a problem," I said with a huff.

"Organic Chem has a lot of formulas and structures to remember. Not many people do well in this class the first time around," Hudson pointed out.

"The *first* time?" I cried. "How many times do people take this class? I can't just give up and try again. I need to pass this class, Hudson," I said, slamming my hand on the table in frustration.

Hudson looked at me, a little surprised at my outburst, then tried to school his face. I could see the corner of his mouth twitching like he was going to smile at my pain. "I'll see what I can do. If you're that determined, we might be able to pull this off. I would just recommend not getting lost and missing another class."

"He told you about that?" I said, hiding my face in my hands. *Lord, Hudson must think I'm a disaster, not only am I bombing this class, he knows I can't find my way out of a paper bag.*

"Jay is a man of few words, so I only got the basics of the situation. He thought I might be able to help you find a way to do some extra credit work based on the situation."

My head popped up, and I looked at him with hope. "Could you do something like that?"

"I might be able to ask that you assist me in my own research; I need a lab assistant. We could call it an even trade; I'll help you with classwork if you take the time to help me out around the lab."

I wanted to jump across the table and hug him for the gift he was giving me, but I held myself back knowing that he probably wouldn't appreciate it. He didn't strike me as the type who liked unwanted physical contact.

"Thank you so much, Hudson, truly, you don't know what this means to me," I said, trying to make sure he heard my sincerity.

"My pleasure. Jay doesn't ever ask for favors, and you seem ready and willing to put in the hard work to catch up," Hudson said, shrugging his shoulders. "Let's start with the hydrocarbons; you keep mixing up the different types, which is part of your problem."

Over the next hour, Hudson and I worked slowly through what he felt were the biggest things I was missing. He was easy to understand and never seemed bothered when I didn't get it right away. He broke down every composition and made sure I knew all the elements and understood how they worked together. I was amazed at how effortless this was for him and how he could make it seem so simple. He even helped me draw out compositions so I could have a reference when I was working on my homework. When our hour was up, his phone started to beep, letting us know we needed to pack it up for the day.

"What days work best for you to meet up?" Hudson asked.

"Tuesdays and Thursdays are my light days."

"Why don't we do Tuesdays working on classwork and Thursdays you can help me in the lab? That way, we can do practical application from what you're learning, it will make more sense to you if you can see it in action."

"Sounds good to me. My last class on those days is at two, so I can do anything after that."

"Why don't we stick to four, that works best with my schedule, and I can block out this room for the rest of the semester. Not many people come at this time, since it's so close to dinner time." He held the door open for me.

"Awesome, I really can't thank you enough for all of this," I said, biting my bottom lip, still feeling embarrassed.

"Really, it's no problem. I have to admit that I was very intrigued to meet a person who got Jay to carry on a conversation long enough to even have him offer my help." He smiled as we headed down the hall.

I laughed, remembering how he didn't speak to me for the first half of our interaction. "I did notice he is a man of few words. I wasn't sure if he was going to take me back to school or chop me up into little bits in the field."

As we made it back to the first floor, a girl walked by but apparently didn't see me and knocked into me, causing me to spill all my books.

"Oops, sorry," she said, then flashed a smile to my left. "Hi, Hudson, what brings you into the main library?"

I rolled my eyes as I bent down to gather my books and was surprised when another set of hands was also doing the same thing. I glanced over and saw Hudson ignoring the girl talking to him while he helped me. I took the books from him and stood up, unsure of what to do since the girl was still waiting for an answer.

"I was tutoring, Mallory," Hudson stated.

Mallory's eyebrows went up, and the shocked look on her face was priceless. Then it quickly turned into an angry scowl. "You never offered to help me study."

"Why would I have done that? You were Parker's girlfriend, but that doesn't mean anything to me," Hudson said flatly.

Now it was my turn to be shocked, I looked at the girl with new eyes. She was tall, slender, legs for days, and a face that could have made her a model. She was not at all like someone I would have pictured Parker dating. Not that I cared, really. We were just friends. I had no right to feel this flare of jealousy at the fact that I was the opposite of everything she was.

"No need to be a prick, Hudson. I know you never liked us dating," Mallory snapped.

"That's where you're wrong. I had no problem with you two dating. What I had a problem with was you making moves on me while dating him."

Holy shit! She tried to cheat on Parker with Hudson? I truly had no idea how close the guys were to each other, but from the looks of it, it was enough to piss Hudson off.

"Come on, Lailah. If we don't head to the cafeteria soon, there won't be anything good left," Hudson said, gently grabbing my elbow and leading me out of the library.

Confused, I let him lead me away without saying anything. *I don't remember agreeing to eat dinner with him.* I looked up at Hudson and saw the anger in his eyes as we walked in silence out into the quad.

"Hudson, are you okay?" I asked, turning to him as I felt him drop his hand from my arm.

He pushed his glasses up on his head and rubbed his eyes as if trying to scrub them clean. "Sorry about that, I hope I didn't make you feel uncomfortable."

"No, you're fine. I'm glad I could be an excuse to get you away from her," I said, knowing what it felt like to be cornered by someone you didn't want to talk to.

Hudson looked at me with an appreciative smile. "Since I dragged you all the way over here, would you like to eat with me? You don't have to if you don't want to, I wouldn't want to put you in an awkward position."

"Sure, I'll join you, wouldn't want to leave you alone in case she comes back," I said, grinning at him, trying to lighten the mood.

Fourteen

Hudson

I was worried that eating dinner with Lailah would be strained after our encounter with Mallory. Surprisingly, it turned out to be the highlight of my day. Conversation seemed to flow smoothly between us after a few halting steps in the beginning. I was amazed to see that she had any interest in hearing about the thesis project I was working on. Most people's eyes glazed over, but she was willing to try and follow, even if she didn't understand half of what I was talking about.

"So, you're telling me that you're working on a solution that can be used to help detect pancreatic cancer?"

"That is the simplest way to explain it, yes. This is one of the few forms of cancer that we can't test for with early detection. Most cases are found when it's too late, and there's no chance of survival," I answered, smiling, pleased that she was getting the gist of what I was doing.

She shook her head, sending her golden curls wild around her shoulders. "That is crazy ambitious for a thesis project."

"My parents own one of the largest pharmaceutical companies in the eastern hemisphere. Compared to what they work on, this project is small time. I grew up with dinner topics that would make the average kid cry from the complexity."

"Man, holiday gatherings with your family must be something else. Do you have siblings? Are they joining in on the family business too?"

"I'm the oldest of three, my brother and sister are still in high school. My sister Grace is projected to graduate a year early and will also be going to school to work in the medical world. She wants to work with patients, though. She is probably the most social out of the whole family. Ben, my brother, is a senior and wants to study biomedical engineering when he graduates." I paused, hating the uncomfortable feeling I get when I have to share about my parents. "Three years ago, my parents separated, they still own the business together, but they work separately. It was not an amicable divorce, but they knew if they split the company, they would lose too many clients."

"Wow, that must have been hard on you," Lailah said, her soul-penetrating eyes filled with concern for me.

I was glad to see her gaze wasn't filled with pity like most people when they heard. I'd known for years before they split that my parents didn't like each other. They no longer hid their fights from us.

"Enough on that topic," I said, waving a hand trying to move on from the subject. "I've taken up far too much of your evening. I'm sure you have better things to do than sit here with me."

She looked down at her watch, and I saw her eyebrows shoot up. "Shit! It can't be this late already." Looking back up, she gave me a guilty smile. "I do need to head back and get some work done, I have a paper to finish for my English class tomorrow."

"Of course, I wouldn't want to hold you back from your schoolwork. What kind of tutor would I be doing that?" I said.

I was surprised when she laughed at my words. I hadn't meant them to be funny, but when I played them over in my head, I understood where she could see the humor in them.

"I know we said to meet up Thursdays for lab work together, but I already have an obligation tomorrow," Lailah said as we walked our trays to the drop off area.

"Not a problem, we will just plan to meet up next Tuesday. Feel free to reach out if you get stuck on something; I might be able to talk you through it," I said, not wanting her to think she had to wait a whole week.

"You're awesome, Hudson," she said as she gave me a quick side hug as we exited the cafeteria. Then she took off toward her dorm.

My arm tingled with electricity where she'd touched me. It was stronger than when I'd first made contact with her as I shook her hand in greeting. I first thought this was a reaction of my power to my anger at being cornered by Mallory. Now I knew that it was Lailah who was giving off the energy, but I couldn't figure out why.

"Thanks for helping her," Jay said at my left, making me jump.

"God, Jay, stop doing that shit to me," I growled. I hate when he sneaks up on me..

Jay just gave me a disapproving side-eye but didn't say anything more.

"Why are you here?" I asked.

"Check your phone," Jay commented.

I pulled my cell out of my backpack, and sure enough, I had a few missed calls and texts. I unlocked it and scrolled through what I had missed.

The first one was from Beth an hour ago.

Beth: **Hudson, I need you and Jay to assist in patrolling. The demons are getting worse and only two of you a night isn't working.**

Beth: **Hudson, I need you to answer that you got my message. It's unlike you to be unresponsive.**

Followed by another twenty minutes later.

Beth: **I am sending Jalen to find you if you don't answer this text in the next five minutes and he has my full permission to stop you from doing whatever is causing you to ignore me.**

Jay: **location?**

Jay's simple demand for my whereabouts. Though I never got to answer it, seeing as he was standing next to me.

"What's got Beth so worked up?" I asked, looking up from my phone.

Jay signaled for me to follow him, not wanting to talk around so many people. I trailed after him until we made it to the parking lot, and I saw his Jeep, which was more like a tank than a car, waiting at the curb. I jumped into the passenger side while he started the engine, causing the car to rumble with its diesel engine.

"There was a flare of demonic energy on the school grounds. They think something is trying to create a portal," Jay informed me.

"That can't happen while we have the wards up."

"They're failing faster, too much demon activity."

"What are we supposed to do about it?"

"Beth wants us to do recon and get more information before we do anything."

"Ah brains and brawn at it again," I said, using Parker's nickname for us.

We rode in silence for a while before I couldn't let the question that I'd wanted to ask him wait any longer. "Why did you give her my number?"

"Fuck if I know." Jay sighed.

For Jay, this response was the equivalent of freaking out. Jay didn't do unknowns, he dealt in strategy, calculated responses, and practicality. The fact that he had no idea why he did what he did must have been throwing him for a loop.

"I needed to help her. I don't know why, but I couldn't just walk away from her when I could help," Jay finally said after I didn't press the matter.

I didn't have a chance to question him further about that since we had reached the area where our sensors had picked up the demon activity. Jay handed me a tablet with a beacon flashing on it once we got out of the Jeep. I looked around and found that we were in the same field where Micah and Brayden had dispatched a lesser demon last week. I headed off in the direction the map was showing, with Jay's silent presence at my side.

It didn't take us long to find the spot we were looking for. The ground was scorched where the demon had tried to get the portal to open and had failed, as evidenced by the charred husk of remains. I squatted down and examined the ground, looking for the portal marking that would tell us where the other side of this was. Unfortunately, the body was sitting on top of it, and I was loath to move it myself. I looked up at Jay with a raised eyebrow. Jay grunted, and with a flick of his hand, a small dust devil of wind wrapped around the remains and lifted it up and away.

"Thank you," I said absently as I worked on deciphering the runes that were now visible.

I took the stylus out of the tablet and started to copy down what I saw so I could send it back to Beth and the others. I knew the typical symbols we studied, but I found a few that I had never seen before. I frowned as I noticed that the spell almost worked—if the almost complete circle was anything to go by. Our wards were barely able to prevent this portal from being opened. What kept bothering me was that the body of the demon that had been left behind wouldn't have been strong enough to make this kind of portal.

"Jay, you haven't seen anything close to a mid-level demon show up on your patrols, have you?"

"No, they've all been lesser demons, but way more than ever before," Jay said.

"We need to head back. I'll need Mr. Creed's help to decipher these new runes." I stood up and sent a text to make sure both Beth and Mr. Creed would be there when we got back.

"This is bad, isn't it?" Jay asked.

I looked up at him in surprise. He was never one to be all doom and gloom, that was Micah's department.

"If we can't figure out how the demons are breaching our wards, they will fail, and we'll have no defense against them," I answered.

Fifteen

Lailah

The day seemed to be passing so slowly, yet way too fast. I was excited to finally get a chance to hang out with Brayden, but I was also freaking out about it. *Was this a date? Should I change into something nicer than my T-shirt and jeans? Would we even have stuff to talk about?* Granted, I thought the same thing last night when I was sitting with Hudson for dinner, but that turned out to be a great time. I was excited to start working with him in his lab next Thursday. It was so cool that he was doing something so amazing; I couldn't even dream of being able to do anything that important for the human race.

"Lala, watch out!" Cami called out, but it was too late.

I crashed into someone who was walking out of the building and carrying a huge stack of books. The books went flying, and I crashed to the ground hard on my ass while the other person landed with a grunt. Once the books and papers fluttered to the ground and I reoriented myself, I found an angry older gentleman scowling at me.

"Do you not have eyes in your head, girl?" the man snapped as he worked to get his large form off the ground.

I scrambled to my feet and reached out a hand to help him to his feet. He slapped it away and sputtered something about being fat but not an invalid.

"I'm so sorry, sir," I apologized as I started to gather up the papers and books.

I looked down and found a sheet covered in strange symbols that gave me the willies. As I handed the books over, I noticed most of them were on the occult. *Who is this guy?* I had never seen this man before, but I didn't know all the teachers at the school. What class could he be teaching with such strange material?

"Mr. Creed, I apologize for my friend, Lailah. She's such a ditz sometimes," Cami said, brushing off the man's black suit jacket.

Something about what she said had him looking sharply at me, but it was more of a curious look than an angry one.

"Yes, well, no harm done. Next time, pull your attention from your phone and watch where you're walking young lady," Mr. Creed said before he continued to his original destination.

I opened my mouth to tell him that I wasn't on my phone, but Cami elbowed me in the ribs causing me to gasp instead. "What the hell, Cami?"

"Trust me when I say not to argue with that man. He knows more about arcane arts and voodoo shit than anyone I know. He could hex you in your sleep, and you would never know," Cami said seriously.

I rolled my eyes. "I don't believe in that crap, no one can take a strand of my hair and curse me. That shit only works if you give it power."

"I wouldn't be too sure about that, Lala," Cami said before linking arms with me and dragging me away.

"Where are we going?" I asked.

"You have your date with Brayden today, right?"

"Yeah, I meet up with him at the coffee shop in two hours."

"Perfect just enough time for you to change."

"What's wrong with my outfit? I put a lot of thought into it," I grumbled. "I'm even wearing a skirt."

"I know you tried, darling, but you are going to have a public date at school with one of the most sought-after bachelors here. You need to knock 'em dead," Cami said with an evil grin on her lips.

"Wait, what?" I said, trying to follow what she was going on about.

"If you want the other girls to leave you alone, you need to show them you have every right to be hanging out with those guys. You're my best friend, but if you like to hang out with those idiots, then I'm going to have to help you. This is the first step in showing your dominance in the female world. You have a bangin' body, use it," Cami declared.

I decided it was better to just do as I was told than to fight Cami when she got like this. We made it back to the dorm, but she dragged me into her room instead of mine. I was shocked when I found the room was spotless, but I was even more shocked to see Maggs from the house party sitting on the couch.

"Hey girl," Maggs said, waving her hand in greeting.

"Hi" was all I had time to say before Cami was throwing clothes at me. "Cami, what is all this?"

"Maggs was kind enough to share some of her clothes with you for this event. She's much closer to your size than I am, so no need to worry about busting out of the tops," Cami said, winking at me.

I blushed, as she so casually called me out about something I tried to hide.

"As much as we all appreciate Cami's eclectic style, she has no idea how to dress a classic woman," Maggs said, standing up and walking over to me. "I, on the other hand, know how to create sex appeal without showing too much skin."

I gulped as I took in Maggs' retro-glam style that matched her figure and her bright-red hair. There was no way I could pull off the confidence she had in those clothes. Truthfully, she was one of those girls who could be wearing a garbage bag and still look stunning.

"None of that," Maggs said as she tapped me on the nose, surprising me out of my thoughts. "You are gorgeous, and I don't want you to think any less of yourself. I found what makes me happy in my own skin, same with Cami. What we're looking for is what you need to wear to feel confident. Each woman wears her clothes like armor; we need to find your battle gear, love," Maggs said with a grin.

I smiled back at her, excited to see what she had brought for me to try. It took us about four outfits till I decided on one that I knew would be perfect for this occasion. It was a maroon sweater dress that fit my body snugly from neck to knees. The game changer for this dress was the back had a deep V that showed off the contrast of the rich color and my pale skin. I felt like I could stare down anyone in this outfit. I pulled my hair into a high pony, so it didn't cover the dramatic effect of the back.

"Now for the shoes, I would say heels, but something tells me that you won't agree," Maggs said, giving me a knowing look.

"You're right, I wouldn't be able to do that, I might break an ankle if I tried," I said, shivering at the thought.

"Would you be willing to try wedges? I find they're easier to walk in," Cami suggested.

I shrugged my shoulders. "Why not, this is about trying new things, right?"

Slipping my feet into the simple ankle booties, I took a few steps and grinned when I didn't die. I looked up and found them both clapping for my success. Cami looked down at her watch and gasped.

"Damn, we have fifteen minutes to get you to the coffee shop," Cami said, grabbing my arm and jerking me out of the room.

"Thanks for everything, Maggs!" I called as we headed down the hall.

Letting Cami set the pace, I followed as best I could on the new shoes. It took all my concentration to keep from toppling over when we hit the steps outside the dorm.

"Cami, slow down. This does me no good if I show up with a broken leg," I snapped, pulling my arm from her.

I stopped, took a deep breath, smoothed out my dress, and then started walking confidently over to the school. Cami walked at my side, making sure I didn't trip and die on the way.

"So, Maggs . . ." I ventured, looking at her out of the corner of my eye.

Cami's cheeks pinked, and she shoved her hands into the pocket of her bright-blue hoodie. "She's a friend, Lala."

"Right, how long is that going to last?" I asked, pushing her.

"I don't know, we haven't gotten that far yet. We're taking things slow, hanging out and stuff," Cami said, kicking a stone off the path.

"I know I haven't known you for long, but I never thought I would see the day that someone made you blush," I teased.

Cami sighed, stopping as her shoulders sagged. "I haven't been in a relationship for a long time. The last time didn't end well. I'm just not sure I'm ready."

I wrapped my arms around Cami and hugged her tightly. "You deserve to be happy. If Maggs can do that for you, then I give her my approval."

"Thanks, Lala," she said, returning my hug. "Now, let's get your sexy self to your date."

We both laughed, and as quickly as I could manage, we made it to the quad. I gave Cami another quick hug, and we parted ways. Taking a deep breath, I squared my shoulders and made my way across the quad to the coffee shop. Thankfully, at this time in the afternoon, it wasn't too busy, and I got in line to order my coffee. When I reached the register, I ordered my chai latte, but when I was about to hand over my money, someone else reached across me with their bank card.

"I would like to pay for the lady's drink," Brayden said, suddenly standing next to me.

I blinked at him a moment then felt my cheeks heat with my blush. "Thank you."

"Of course, it's my pleasure." Brayden smiled, making my heart skip a beat. "I saved us some seats over by the window if that's okay with you."

"Sounds great," I said as he led me over with a gentle hand on my elbow.

"You look amazing," Brayden whispered in my ear as I sat down in one of the large overstuffed chairs.

My heart pounded in my chest as his words registered, sending a ripple of energy over my skin. My tongue stuck to the roof of my mouth as it went dry, and I was left unable to answer him. Thankfully, the barista called out my drink was ready, and he walked over to get it for me.

Pull it together, Lailah! It's been a long time since a guy has shown he is interested in you, so don't blow it.

Brayden came back with my drink and handed it to me as he sat across from me. Apparently, he had been there long enough before me to already have a drink, which he picked up and took a sip from as he let his eyes wander over me. Trying to act normal, I took a large gulp of my drink and was rewarded with burning my tongue and wincing at the pain, causing me to cough.

"Careful, it's hot! Do you need me to get you some water or something?" Brayden asked, leaning forward, worried.

I waved my hand as he tried to stand. "No, I'm fine, just didn't test it before taking a drink."

"There's no rush on my end. I have the whole evening free," Brayden said, settling back into his chair.

"Oh, I guess I don't have much going on tonight either except for homework, but who doesn't," I said, feeling a little awkward.

"What piece of the school did you decide on for your University 101 class?"

"The chapel. I remembered hearing about how Ryevick used it to get the church off his back so the school could run the way he wanted it to," I said, remembering that was when I'd met Brayden for the first time. "I've also been doing a side project on the Elementi."

Brayden choked on his coffee. After taking a moment to compose himself, he looked up at me. "Why would you be looking into that?"

"Come on, you're telling me that you wouldn't want to know more about a secret group of the Knights Templar? Professor Phillips even gave me access to the special archives room. I found the stuff about the chapel, but I also found a lot more about the Elementi. I was talking to Cami about what I learned and the strange things that happened around them. Something she said made me think of the story you told me about the fountain," I said, excited.

"What would the fountain have in common with the Elementi? Aiden Ryevick was born way after the Knights' golden era."

"Yes, but this Elementi group didn't get started until the end of the Knights' peak. What if Ryevick was part of this splinter group? He might not have been as crazy as people think he was," I said, sharing for the first time the thoughts that had been rolling around in my head.

Brayden set his cup down and leaned into me like he was going to share a secret. "Let's say he was, do you think this group is still around today?"

I sighed and shook my head, sitting back. "No, I think that the group died off. The strange happenings that came with their involvement died out during the Victorian age when coal took the world by storm."

"I have to say that I'm quite impressed with your detective skills. Maybe you need to change from a history major to something in criminal justice."

I grinned at him. "You tease, but when I get interested in something, I can't seem to let it go, especially when it's history related."

"So how would someone find himself gaining your interest?" Brayden asked, a smoldering look in his eyes.

"Seeing that it only happened once before, it won't be easy." I decided to leave off that once I'd been an idiot, letting myself be used and left when he was done.

"Nothing worth having is ever easy," Brayden said, looking me over.

I never would have guessed that Brayden would have this side to him. He had struck me as a go-with-the-flow kind of guy. I guess even the mellow guys have a wild streak in them.

"How are your studies going?" I asked, trying to change the topic. I wasn't sure how much more sexual tension I could handle in public.

"We're working on a project to find the best way to help restore forests after wildfires. It happens all over the world, and it's one of the hardest things to control, but what we do with it after it happens is as important as controlling the burn."

"That's cool; we didn't have that problem where I grew up. Wisconsin gets lots of rain, so everything stays really lush and green," I said, thinking about the forest fires I'd heard about in other states and how devastating they were.

"The Student Council is working on our Halloween party in three weeks. We always do some big gathering since it will be right before cracking down for midterms."

"No way. That's awesome. Does everyone dress up?"

"Those who want to can, but it's not required, although lots of people do. Everyone here likes to let loose."

"Do you dress up?" I asked, not sure I could picture him dressed up in some silly costume.

"I dressed up last year," Brayden admitted.

He was not going to make this easy. "As?"

"Guess you'll have to go with me to find out," Brayden said with a wink.

I laughed, seeing how he'd played me. "Sounds good to me."

"No fair. I was going to ask her to go with me." Parker's voice came from behind me.

I turned and saw him dragging a chair over and sitting next to me. I looked over at Brayden, unsure of what to do. Brayden's answer to Parker joining us was to move the small table between us and drag my chair over closer to him.

"Sorry, Parker, but Lailah and I were having a private conversation," Brayden said, glaring.

"Sorry, but you're in a public place, and I'm allowed to sit where I want," Parker said, scooting to my other side.

"Um, I can go if you need to talk to Brayden about something," I said, trying not to fidget while stuck between them.

"No, Trouble. That's not the problem. Brayden just needs to learn how to share time with friends," Parker said, patting my hand that was gripping my dress. "So, did I hear correctly that you're going to the Halloween shindig?"

"Brayden was just telling me about it, I don't see any reason not to go," I answered, trying to stay neutral when I saw Hudson walking over to us.

"Hey, Lailah, guys. I didn't know you all knew each other," Hudson said as he pulled a chair to join our group.

"I had the pleasure of meeting Lailah on her first week here; we bumped into each other in town," Parker said, puffing out his chest.

"If crashing into me and crushing my cookie is what you call *bumping into each other.*" I snorted.

"Come on, are you ever going to let that go?" he whined.

I ignored him and looked over at Hudson, "Brayden, like Jay, rescued me from wandering around the school grounds lost during the school tour."

"Wait, when did you meet Jay?" Parker butted in again. "Trouble, you been keeping secrets?"

I laughed. "It's hardly a secret. I got lost going on a run, and Jay found me and brought me back to the school grounds. He's also the one who gave me Hudson's number to tutor me."

"Well, it seems you've met all of us now," Brayden said.

I quickly counted each interaction. "Huh, you're right. I didn't notice that till you just said it."

After a bit, all the guys seemed to relax, and we all chatted comfortably with each other. I noticed that even though they all lived together, it didn't seem like they really *knew* each other. I was laughing at something Parker said when the sprinklers in the coffee shop went off, and the blare of a fire alarm filled the room. Parker grabbed my wrist, pulling me out of my chair and ushered me out before I even realized what was going on. Brayden followed on our heels, and I felt his hand on my lower back, making sure I didn't get knocked over by others running out of the cafe.

"You alright?" Hudson asked once we found an open space to stop.

"Yeah, a little damp but no worse for wear," I said, trying to brush the water droplets off my dress. "What happened?"

"I'm not sure, but I'm sure we'll hear about it later," Brayden said, brushing his damp hair out of his face.

I felt internal heat rise as I noticed the light-blue T-shirt he had on was sticking to his chest, showing his well-defined muscles. Trying not to stare, I looked over at Parker, whose back was to me as he was taking his shirt all the way off. The muscles that moved along his sculpted back made my mouth water.

"Lailah," Hudson said, putting a gentle hand on my shoulder.

"Hmm?" I said, turning to look at him after being caught ogling Parker.

"Do you want one of us to walk back to your dorm with you?" Hudson repeated with a knowing glint in his blue eyes.

"Nope. I mean, I'm good; it's not that far, honestly," I said, trying to pull my scrambled thoughts together.

"After hearing how often you seem to get lost, I just wanted to make sure."

"Thanks, Hudson, really, but I actually have gotten much better," I said, grinning.

"If you say so, Trouble. Call one of us if you get lost so we can send out the search party," Parker said, and I could feel his body heat from behind me.

I looked up at him, smiling. "You got it."

I waved at them all and made my way back to my dorm, grinning at how the evening had turned out.

Brayden

When I got back to the house, I headed directly to Micah's room. When I reached it, I didn't even knock before I walked in. I found Micah lying on his bed with his obnoxious red headphones on and his foot tapping to the beat. Walking over to him, I grabbed his phone and unplugged the headphones. Quickly stepping back out of reach, I watched as he bolted upright with murder in his eyes.

"Who the fuck," Micah spluttered before his gaze landed on me. "Brayden, what the hell man?"

I walked over to his desk and rolled his computer chair over and sat down facing him. "Remember when you told me that you met Synergy, and I laughed it off?"

"Yeah . . ."

"Well, I'm listening."

"What happened? Something must have changed for you to believe me now."

"I just had a coffee date with Lailah, the one you ran into that night we killed the demon in the bathroom."

"You're telling me about your dating life, why?"

"Because I ended that date with Parker and Hudson joining us."

"Okay, that's awkward, but I don't get the correlation here, Bray."

"I spent an hour with them after they crashed our date, and I wasn't pleased, but I also didn't want to chop their dicks off for interfering. We all had a good time and didn't bicker once after we got settled. Not to mention that Lailah is leaking elemental energy like crazy."

Micah grinned. "You sure it was energy she was leaking?"

"Shut the fuck up, you know what I'm talking about. I just didn't connect it, but Lailah is the one you met in the library, isn't she?"

"Yeah, that's why I was so thrown off when I ran into her again that same night. It seemed odd that the demon was trying to get in the dorm, but when I thought about it, I think they're going after her."

After Micah dropped that bomb, I was glad I was sitting. Holy shit, it all made sense. The demons were trying to get to her before we did. I sat up and jumped to my feet.

"Where are you going?" Micah called after me.

"We need a family meeting *now*," I said, pulling out my phone and scrolling to the group text Beth had created, but we hardly ever used.

Me: **Meeting in the library in 10 min this is NOT an option, Synergy has been found and is in danger.**

Parker: **WTF Brayden you're joking, right?**

Beth: **Brayden what is the meaning of calling this meeting. You need to run these things by me.**

Beth texted me privately. I knew I was going to piss her off doing it, but I was more worried about Lailah and the unknown danger that she was in.

Jay: **Already there.**

"Brayden, are you trying to get Beth to salt your Wheaties with a stunt like that? You know she takes her role way too seriously," Micah said, jogging up to me.

Shrugging my shoulders, I pushed open the door to the library and came face-to-face with the woman, her hands on her hips and a look that told me I was in for a tongue-lashing.

"Brayden Dolton, what the hell is the meaning of this?"

Beth was our mother while we lived here at school. She ran the house and made sure we had everything we needed. She was also the person in charge of training the new generation of Elementi Warriors.

"Like I said, we found Synergy, and she's in danger. We need to protect her before the demons get to her," I said, cutting to the chase, knowing I couldn't bullshit Beth.

"How could you possibly know about her?" Beth asked, letting out a breath.

"You knew?" Micah snapped, catching us all off guard.

Micah was one of the loudest to mock Synergy's existence, so for him to be upset about it was something I didn't see coming. I figured he would have been happy if we never found Synergy and were able to let this task die out.

"I'll explain when the others get here," Beth said as she walked over to the couch and took a seat.

I gripped Micah's shoulder and then walked over to take a seat and wait for the other two. Jay was already in one of the leather armchairs with what looked like files in his lap. He must have been working on something for his dad. We didn't have to wait long for Parker and Hudson to join us. I knew they were somewhere in the house since we all walked back together after hanging out with Lailah.

"How should we start this?" Beth asked, looking at me.

"Did you know that Synergy was human, female, and here, attending school?" I demanded.

Beth nodded her head, looking at all of us before she spoke. "Yes, we found her and brought her to the school on a scholarship."

"Brayden, what are you guys talking about?" Hudson inquired.

"It would seem that the reason for the rise in demon activity is because Synergy is here at the school, trickling elemental energy all over the place," I explained.

"Talk about dropping a bomb! Hell, Beth, why didn't you say anything?" Parker said, running his hands through his hair.

"She has no idea who or what she is. I wanted her here so we could keep her safe and give her a chance to learn about us. I purposely helped make sure that many of her teachers were Elementi and could direct her to find out about us on her own, before we brought her into the fold," Beth said, laying it all out for us.

"Who is it?" Jay demanded.

"Lailah," I answered.

The room went into chaos at that final piece of the puzzle.

"What the actual fuck, Beth!"

"How could you leave her to fend for herself like that?"

"How long till you were going to tell us?"

"What the hell are we going to do now?"

"Enough!" Beth commanded, silencing everyone. "Keep in mind that she was raised in the states with a normal family, and she has no idea that this is even a possibility for her. You were all told about the idea of being an Elementi Warrior from birth. Imagine the shock she would face if we just pulled her in cold turkey."

"She knows more than you give her credit for," I said, thinking back on our conversation.

"Phillips has been keeping me apprised of her interest and what she has figured out. I also have Cami as her personal guardian, who is also letting me know her findings," Beth informed us.

"That's how you got Cami to come back," Parker said, connecting the dots.

Beth nodded. "I needed the best guardian for her, and Cami is one of our elites."

"At the rate her power is building, she's going to crack sooner rather than later. How are you going to deal with her coming into her powers now that she's around all of us?" Hudson asked.

"I knew keeping you all away from her wasn't going to work, but I had to try," Beth said, rubbing the back of her neck.

"That's why you kept it from us," Micah stated.

"Yes, the more she's around you, the faster her power will awaken. It's also causing the demons to come in greater numbers because they can taste her power." Beth looked at all of us before she continued, "The only way to contain her powers is for her to bond with the group."

"So, this is what it's come to," Micah said bitterly. "I have to give over control of my powers to a directionally-challenged, doe-eyed, country bumpkin."

"Shut the hell up, Micah, you don't even know her," Parker growled.

Micah smirked at him. "Well, it seems like you have already become the perfect pet without even getting the benefits."

Parker jumped to his feet and charged at Micah. I met Jay's gaze and gave him a nod, right before a gust of wind shoved Parker to the other side of the room, pinned to the wall.

"Don't think you're safe with your fancy trick, Jay. I would be careful when you fall asleep tonight. No telling who might take control of your body," Parker taunted.

"Parker Jones, do not make me put you in a void room tonight because, so help me God, I will do it," Beth barked.

At this threat, he sagged against the wall, surrendering, and Jay released his hold. I dropped my head into my hands. Now we had all the information, but we were no better off in understanding how to handle the fact that Synergy was found and had already worked her way into our lives.

"I'm sure it may come as a surprise to you all, but I do have a plan in the works," Beth said once everyone had calmed back down. "I have been in charge of making sure you all get trained and prepared for the battles to come since you all came into your powers. I know how to handle Lailah."

"It's not that we don't have faith in your abilities, Beth. Lord knows you have been through it with all of us," Hudson said, rubbing his chin thinking. "Synergy is an unknown. We all know what each of the five is capable of, but we know so little about Synergy. If she is to be the axis that we all pivot from, we need to be around her. That portal attempt almost worked; we need to keep her safe until you decide to bring her here to The Manor."

"I agree with Hudson, Lailah is a walking accident," Parker said. "I think we need to be around her more. If the demons are getting worse, then we need to be ready for something bigger to happen."

I looked around the room, wondering if anyone else was aware that this was the first time that we were working toward a common goal. Typically, after an outburst like Parker's, Micah would have stormed off not to be seen for the rest of the night. Now here we all were, trying to hold it together to make sure Lailah was safe.

Beth seemed to contemplate this suggestion a moment before she answered, "How do we do this without making it seem strange? I've already had to back Cami off, so she doesn't think it's suspicious that her best friend never leaves her alone."

"I'll get her to run with me in the morning," Jay said. The room froze in shock.

Beth coughed surreptitiously before nodding her head. "That would kill two birds with one stone. It will help to burn off some of her energy and not have her sitting in one location for too long."

"I'm already meeting up with her Tuesdays and Thursdays for tutoring and lab work," Hudson said.

"I can be around whenever you need me to be; she's used to me popping up at random times," Parker said with a grin directed at me.

"Coordinating with Cami, I'm sure all of us can be around when she feels like she can't," I said, not willing to fall for Parker's bait.

We all turned to Micah, waiting to see what he had to offer.

"Fuck, I'll look after her, but that doesn't mean I have to hang out with her. I can be around if she needs help. I will intervene, but I'm not a damn babysitter," Micah grumbled.

"We can work with that," Beth said, standing up. "I had hoped to give her time to adjust to being in a new school and in a new country before we dropped this all on her. Best laid plans and all. Goodnight, boys; let me know if you need me for anything."

Lailah

"Lala, we have to strike back!" Cami said, slamming her fist on the cafeteria table.

"How would you suggest we do that? Look, it's not that big of a deal. So, I got a little wet, but it really was a fun night, even if the others ended up joining us," I said, smiling at Cami's protective streak.

"Nope, we can't let this slide. Those bitches set the sprinklers off on purpose. How much more are you going to take from them?" Cami badgered.

When Cami found me at our normal spot for lunch, she had been fuming about how some of the girls were telling everyone what happened last night. Apparently, it was another one of their plots to disrupt me hanging out with The Manor boys. I smirked at the fact that I'd been not only hanging out with one, but the top three most-wanted of the bunch.

"This is how I see it. I've already won, they choose to hang out with me and want to be my friend. I didn't have to do anything to get them to like me, except get lost and suck at Organic Chem. You can't change someone's mind when making genuine friendships," I pointed out.

Cami paused and looked at me for a moment like I had just told her I was going to be president. "Look at this, one group date down, and my little Lala is ready to take over the world. Maybe we need to get you more of those dirty books about having all those boyfriends you like."

"Shut up! You promised not to say anything after you found it in my room. I know I had it hidden under my pillow, but I'm not going to ask what you were doing snooping," I grumbled, narrowing my eyes at Cami.

She laughed so hard I was afraid she was going to fall out of her chair. "Oh man, if that's your pissed off face, we're going to need to work on that. It's like a bunny trying to bare its teeth. It just doesn't work."

I picked up my crumpled napkin and chucked it at her, hitting her right in the nose.

"Nice shot," Parker said, sliding in to sit next to me.

Turning to him, I beamed. "Thanks."

"Knock it off, you two. The last thing I need is for you to gang up on me." Cami pouted.

"Stop making such a good target, Cami, and we won't," Parker pointed out.

"You're one to talk. I heard you let Micah get under your skin last night," Cami said with a smirk.

"What happened with Micah?" I asked. I knew that they didn't like each other one bit.

Parker shot Cami a glare before he turned his attention back to me. "Nothing really, all he needs to do is open his mouth, and we have a problem. He is just an ass, and all he cares about is himself."

I didn't have much to say about that, not knowing Micah well. Both he and Jay weren't seen around school very often, if at all. My phone vibrated on the table, showing I had received a text. I made to grab for it, but Parker swooped in and plucked it out of my hand.

"Still no lock screen, I see," Parker said as he started reading my text.

"What the hell, Parker. Give that back. God, Cami's right, you're like a two-year-old," I said, trying to grab my phone.

Not even looking at me, Parker held me off with an arm around my waist while he typed something back.

"You can't answer that! You don't even know what I would have said. Who was it? Come on, Parker, knock it off," I said, lunging at him.

Parker's head had been turned away from me, but just as I made my move, he turned his head back to me. Surprised at my proximity, he didn't hold on to me, and I crashed my forehead into his. His head was harder than concrete, making my eyes water from the impact. I was now draped over the front of him, and when I tried to move off him, I felt him place a gentle kiss to the side of my neck, below my ear. I froze, unsure of what to make of it. *Maybe it was an accident, there's no reason Parker would make a move like that. We're just friends, right? I mean, he saw me on a date with Brayden last night. Oh God, what if that wasn't a date?* Parker grasped my shoulders and gingerly set me back in my seat, looking me over.

"Damn, looks like you're going to have a bruise," Parker said, standing up. "I'm gonna get some ice. I'll be right back."

Unable to say anything, I just sat there, staring at his empty seat. Cami decided to come check on me since I still wasn't moving. She took Parker's seat and rested her chin in her hands, staring up at me. "So, is this where I ask you how many men you want in your harem?"

"What?" I asked, finally regaining the ability to speak.

Cami gave me a toothy grin. "Oh no, Lala. You can't play this off. I totally saw that lip action Parker snuck in there."

"So, it was on purpose?" I asked.

"Hell yeah, it was. That boy just made his move! I have to say, I'm impressed he waited so long. Parker is not one for delayed gratification."

"Last night; that was a date, right? Not just a friend coffee date, but a real date."

"Brayden doesn't do friend dates, look who his best friend is. Why do you ask?"

"If Parker knew I was on a date with Brayden, why would he make a move on me? Oh God, how did this happen?" I said, cradling my head carefully.

"Do you know how many women would kill for one of them to make a move, let alone two of them?!"

"Can we talk about this later when my head isn't having its own drum jam on my brain?" I begged. "Thank God I'm done with classes for the day."

"When he comes back with the ice, I'll walk you back to the dorm, and you can sleep it off. You have the whole weekend to work on homework."

"Sounds like a plan."

"Found an ice pack, sorry it took so long. The nurse was removing a splinter from some kid's ass," Parker said, shoving said ice pack into my hands.

I tentatively placed the pack on my head, and even though it hurt, it also helped. Parker squatted down in front of me, so I didn't have to look up at him.

"I'm really sorry, Trouble, I didn't mean to scramble your brain right before the weekend," he said, squeezing my knee. "Oh yeah, the text was from Jay. He asked if you wanted to try a new running trail tomorrow. I told him you would love to, but I can text him back and tell him your asshole friend took you out of commission."

"No, it's fine. I'll deal with it. I'm sure it will be gone after some ibuprofen," I said, trying not to make him feel worse.

"Come on, Lala, let's get you back to your room before someone else tries to knock you out," Cami said, grabbing my arm.

I kept the ice pack on my head while we walked back to the dorm. Parker was following us like a kicked puppy, and wouldn't stop apologizing. When we reached the steps to the dorm, I turned and frowned at him.

"Parker, enough, I get it. I'm not mad at you about us crashing skulls. It was an accident, but if you keep this up, I'm going to be pissed at you for a whole other reason," I snapped.

Parker's eyes widened at my outburst, and he stood there a little stunned. "Right, okay. I'll leave you alone, but text me if you need anything."

I felt a little guilty about snapping at him, but my head hurt, and all I wanted to do was lie down. The fact that he'd tried to sneak a kiss by me also had me on edge. I didn't know how I was going to handle the situation since I wasn't sure if there was anything really going on with Brayden. I flopped into my bed with the ice pack wrapped in a damp towel.

"Hey, I'm meeting up with my sisters tonight, so I'll be off campus. If you need anything, let me know, but I'm sure you could also reach out to any of the guys if you needed someone right away," Cami teased.

I lifted the towel to glare at her, but she just winked and blew a farewell kiss. I fell into a light sleep filled with strange dreams that seemed to flow from one to another. In one dream, I felt like I was being chased down a hallway by a strange monster.

The hall never seemed to end, and the monster kept getting closer and closer. Just before it was about to get me, I tripped and fell into the next dream.

Now, I was on a dance floor, swaying with the music. I felt someone come up behind me and place their hands on my hips. I looked back to find Parker, his typical playful grin was replaced with one that had more heat behind it. He pulled me against him until there was no space between us from ass up. As I relaxed into his hold, letting the desire in his eyes draw me in, his hands traveled up from my hips and up my sides. I shivered at his touch against my skin. When I looked down, I found I was wearing some crazy tiny top that was more Cami's style than mine. In that moment, though, I was glad for it. I relished the feel of Parker's touch. I closed my eyes to enjoy every moment.

I felt another presence appear in front of me, and before I could open my eyes, I felt lips place a soft kiss on my neck. I moaned, letting my eyes flutter open and found myself looking into Brayden's heated gaze. He pressed his body along my front while Parker kept up his attention from behind, setting my body on fire. Brayden drew my attention back to him by trailing a finger along my jawline, down my neck, and gliding over the swell of my breast. I felt my breath hitch as Parker, not to be outdone, started to nibble on the back of my neck. If I hadn't had both of them holding me up, I wasn't sure my legs would have been up for the challenge.

Brayden slipped his hand into my hair and pulled my face up to him as he took my lips. It was a slow, drawn-out kiss, like he had nowhere else to be but with me. Parker worked over my neck with his teeth while his hands traveled up to my chest. I arched into him as he let his fingers graze over my nipples before he pinched them, making me gasp. Not needing any other encouragement, Brayden slipped his tongue in, teasing me to join him. I'd never kissed anyone like this, so I hesitated, unsure of what he wanted. As if sensing my unease, Brayden adjusted his hold on me and delved deeper into the kiss, taking me along for the ride.

Parker's hands trailed down my chest, kneading along my sides and hips till he reached the border of my pants. He slid one finger on either side, caressing the skin that was still covered. I felt the button of my jeans pop open, and one of his hands slip deeper till he hit what he was looking for. I whimpered as his fingers grazed my clit, sending shocks through my body.

"Moan for us, Lailah," Brayden whispered against my lips.

His words sent heat surging through my body. I quivered at the dirtiness of it, never having had someone say anything like that to me. Parker stroked again, and I moaned in pleasure, my fingers digging into Brayden's arms.

"Oh God," I panted as Parker started to rub two fingers on my needy flesh. "What are you doing to me?"

"Setting you free, Trouble," Parker growled into my ear, his voice thick with his own need.

I tipped my head back and wrapped an arm around his neck to pull him down to me. This time, I was the one who took charge of the kiss, taking all I wanted from him. Brayden freed my breasts from the shirt and took one in his mouth. I cried out at the overstimulation that was coursing along my body.

"Let go, Lailah. Let us set you free; you've been locked away for too long," Brayden said before he took my nipple in his teeth and gently bit down.

It was all I needed to be pushed over the edge, and I was no longer able to support myself as pleasure overtook my body.

I woke up panting, skin covered in a sheen of sweat, and knew by the dampness in my pajamas I had just orgasmed in my dream. *What the fuck just happened?* With a shaky hand, I wiped my forehead, trying to make sense of what I'd just been dreaming. I reached under my pillow and pulled out the book I'd hidden there. I looked at the cover that had a confident woman backed by five guys with whom she was in a relationship at the same time.

That could never work, there is no way that guys would be willing to share one woman in the real world. I thought back to my dream. *Well, it seems that I wouldn't mind if two certain guys could figure out how to share.* I blushed as I remembered their touch on my skin. It had felt so real.

"Time for a cold shower," I mumbled to myself.

Grabbing my shower stuff, I made my way down the hall and breathed a sigh of relief when I found it empty. I really didn't want to deal with the crazy girls who had it out for me. Now, I always made sure to take everything I needed in with me so it didn't wander off. I gently scrubbed my scalp, and combined with the heat of the water, the last of my lingering headache faded. I took the time to shave since there wasn't a demand for the showers at five o'clock in the evening.

"I can't believe he blew you off like that. What has gotten into them lately?" a girl whined.

"Ever since Parker's been hanging out with the charity case, he hasn't been paying attention to anyone else. Did you hear that Hudson is actually tutoring her?" another girl shared. "He even blew off Mallory, and remember how he was so into her last year?"

I frowned, pausing mid-shave of my right leg. Hudson had told me the whole story at dinner that night. The one he shared with me was a seemingly different version than these girls knew. Of course, Mallory wouldn't want to be seen as a cheating whore, but if the shoe fits... Not that Hudson acted on her advances, he was too good a guy to do that to his friend.

"I asked Brayden to go with me to the Halloween party, but he said he was already going with someone. How much you wanna bet it's her?" the first girl said.

"Parker has been turning down everyone, too. Even Hudson said he wasn't going to go with anyone. I know he keeps saying as a TA he needs to focus on school, but he's making time to work with *her* twice a week!" the second girl screeched.

"You know what's crazy, I've even noticed that Micah has been scaring off girls who have been messing with her. I've never heard or seen of him looking out for anyone besides Brayden," the first girl said, sounding confused.

"What's so special about her? I mean, I guess she's kind of pretty, but she isn't even that smart if she needs that much help from a tutor," the second girl grumbled as they left the bathroom.

I quickly finished my shower and hustled out of the bathroom. I peeked out the door first to make sure they weren't still in the hall. I dashed to my room and flopped onto my couch while I processed what I'd just heard. I knew Brayden had asked me to go, and I agreed, but so did Parker, but I never gave him an answer. I didn't think Hudson had said much about it other than he was going. What caught me off guard was what they said about Micah. I didn't think he liked me at all, why would he look out for me from the shadows?

My phone chirped at me from the coffee table. Grabbing it, I saw it was a text from Jay.

Jay: **Parker said he hurt you, you okay?**

I smiled, I liked that he was checking in on me.

Me: **He has a hard head but I survived. Next time, I won't try to headbutt him when he does something stupid.**

Jay: **You still up for running?**

Me: **Totally! What time do you want to meet up?**

Jay: **6?**

I groaned. I was out of my early morning routine thanks to Cami and her love of sleep and late nights.

Me: **I can manage that.**

Jay: **Meet you out front of your dorm. We have to drive to the trail head.**

Me: **Sounds good, see you tomorrow.**

This will be good; I need to get back to running, and it might help keep me from having crazy sex dreams. I shivered at the phantom feeling of their touch. Standing, I shook it off, not wanting to get distracted, and I decided to do some homework. Nothing like working on a psychology project to keep your mind from wandering.

Lailah

I jogged down the steps of the dorm to find a big black Jeep waiting, rumbling as it idled. I peeked up in the window and saw Jay inside, waiting. I opened the door and had to pull myself into the Jeep since it was lifted. I had always wanted a Jeep growing up, but that was before my mother showed me all the reports of people dying in them from rolling over. I didn't think that would happen with Jay, but it kept me from buying one in high school. Jay greeted me with a nod of his head and a small twitch of his lips that was as close to a smile as I guessed he gave. We drove in silence, but it wasn't uncomfortable; it felt tranquil, peaceful. There was no need to fill the car with pointless chatter, the quiet said just as much.

It took about thirty minutes to get where he was taking us. I noticed the open fields and grazing lands faded away to tree-filled hill country. Jay pulled into a small parking lot that looked like it didn't see much traffic. I saw the trail marker for the Lullwater trail, and the map of the trails carved on a large panel of wood. I hopped out of the Jeep and walked around to look at the map. I saw there were a few different trails we could pick from, some longer and some shorter.

"You wanna do a hard trail or a more open trail?" Jay asked.

I woke up to find no lingering issues from the mishap with Parker, so that wasn't a problem. I shook out my body, seeing how it was feeling today. "Let's do something more challenging. I think I need to push it to the max today."

This time Jay really smiled at me, excitement flashing in his eyes. "I was hoping you were going to say that."

He walked to the back of the Jeep and pulled a few things from the trunk. He handed over a vest that had two water bottles on the front for easy access, and the backpack portion had snacks and a water refill sleeve. Jay shouldered what looked more like a military-style pack that clipped around his waist, keeping it snug to his body.

"Wow, you are super prepared for this. What if I'd said I wanted the easy run?" I asked.

Jay looked at me with a small grin as he locked up the car. "You like a personal challenge, and this will definitely give you that." He walked up to me and leaned in to whisper close to my ear. "Also, I think you don't have many people who challenge you like I will."

I stood stunned. He gave a soft chuckle and nudged me with his shoulder to shake me out of my frozen state.

"Have you done any trail running before?" he asked.

Shaking my head, unable to look at him, I messed with the straps for the backpack vest.

"Keep your strides short, you need to be able to dodge and jump at short notice. Keep your gaze a good fifteen feet ahead, so you don't trip." He paused to make sure I understood. "When we run uphill, keep your knees soft, but if it's too rough, don't try to run it, just fall to a fast walk. Downhills, don't land on your heels, keep it soft; otherwise, your knees are going to be screaming tomorrow."

"Got it," I said, hopping up and down a little, shaking out my legs and excited to get this run started.

"Keep up if you can," Jay taunted as he took off down the trail.

I was quick on his heels, keeping in mind what he told me, not getting too close behind him so I could see what was coming. The trail dimmed as we got deeper into the woods, the trees casting shadows across the path, making it harder to tell what to avoid. I trusted my body to respond the way I needed it to and focused more on what was around me. The forest was lush and green, full of animal activity. We reached our first downhill portion, and the decline was steep. A wooden plank had been placed every two feet to give traction as you made your way. Once down, we worked our way around large trees with roots spreading out around them.

I could feel my lungs burning at the effort to keep up with Jay, but I wasn't going to wimp out on this. He'd been right, he laid down the challenge, and I was now going to rise to the occasion. The feel of my blood pumping through my veins and the sweat trickling down my back made me feel so alive. I craved the ability to push my body to use the pent-up energy I had and set it free through my muscles. Jay led the way across a fallen log over a river that was flowing swiftly under my feet.

Jay seemed to float over these obstacles, nothing seemed to faze him. He ran with such a fluid motion; it was like he was flying along the ground. I could see the muscles in his arms tighten as he leaned into the uphill climb, his calves bulging as he pushed away from the rocky step. I was so distracted I almost slid down the hill when rocks shifted under my feet, sending me careening to the right. I caught myself with my hands, but I could feel the rocks biting into my skin. I knew they would be scratched up along with my knee, but I managed to keep from backsliding. I scrambled the rest of the way up the hill—even though it was more like a rock face—and managed to make it to the top without further incident.

Jay was waiting for me at the top, gulping down water as his chest heaved. Good to know I wasn't the only one who was winded from that last part. I brushed the rock from my hands, and some of the cuts started to well up with blood, but I had expected that. I poured some water over them to wash away the last bit of dirt, and they stung, but I would live. Jay walked over and grabbed my wrist, turning over my hand to inspect it himself. When he touched me, I felt a current of energy wash over me, causing me to jerk my hand away from him. He looked at me with a questioning gaze, unsure of my reaction.

"You didn't feel that?" I asked.

"Feel what?" said he asked, taking my hand once again, but this time there was no energy. "Hold still. I've got a first aid kit."

He dropped his pack and started searching through it. Had I been the only one who felt that energy when we touched? Granted, it didn't happen the second time, but it couldn't have been just me. Jay deftly bandaged up my hands and my knee, and we were off again. I assured him I was fine, and we didn't need to head back just because I'd gotten scraped up. The farther in the woods we went, the more breathtaking it became. Never before had I seen such an old forest untouched by human hands. After we ran for another hour or so, I was dripping sweat, and my legs started to tremble.

"Jay, I don't know that I can keep going if we don't take a break soon. We've been running for almost two hours," I said in between gulping breaths.

"Do you think you can make it just a little farther if we take it easy?" Jay asked.

"How far is a little father?" I asked, not trusting him to be honest.

He grinned at me as if he was pleased that I was challenging him. "Just down this hill and to the left a little. It will be worth it."

I groaned, knowing that he was going to win this. "Fine, but if I don't think it's worth it, then you owe me a foot massage."

"What do I get if it is?" Jay asked.

I paused, unsure of what he would want. "What do you want?"

"You, running with me every morning for a week," Jay answered.

"Really?! That's what you want? Sure, I'm fine with that," I said, surprised that was his choice.

"Let's get a move on then," Jay said as he disappeared down the hill.

"Come on, Lailah. You can do this," I said, trying to get a little pep in my step.

I made my way down the hill, which was steeper than any we had managed to this point. I was glad there were rocks embedded into the trail, so I didn't end up sliding down it on my butt. When I got to the bottom, I hung a left where the trail split, like Jay had said, and followed along a small stream. The going was rough, like animals, and not people, used this path. I had to manage every step carefully, so I didn't twist my ankle and end up not making it back to school at all. Just when I was about to give up and just sit right there on the path, I turned another corner around a stand of trees and gasped.

The grove of trees opened up to show a waterfall that was shooting out of a rock wall ahead of me. The water splashed into a pool of water that fed the stream we'd been running alongside. The cool mist of the waterfall felt like heaven on my sweaty skin, refreshing me. I felt a breeze weaving through the trees, sweeping up the mist, causing the sun to reflect in it, creating a giant rainbow. The wind swirled around me, wrapping me in the prism of colors before it dissipated.

"So, I guess we're going to see each other a lot this week," Jay said, appearing behind me, making me jump.

"Ah! Don't do that, stomp your feet or something, will you," I said, clutching my chest.

Jay just grinned and made his way over to an open area with a fallen tree. He slipped off his backpack and sat down and began pulling out food.

"You thought of everything, didn't you," I said, joining him.

"It's always smart to be prepared," Jay said, handing me a white paper bag.

"How could you possibly know to bring these?" I said, looking into the bag, confirming that they were indeed my favorite sugar cookies.

"You forget, I live with Parker," Jay said, shrugging. "He felt bad and gave me these for you, said it would make you forgive him."

I laughed so hard I almost knocked myself off the log into the dirt. Parker knew just how much I loved these cookies.

"I'm going to assume from your reaction that his guess was correct."

"These cookies could get anyone back in my good graces," I said, pulling one out and breaking it in half. "Wanna try some?"

Jay tentatively reached out and took the chunk of cookie. "Normally, I don't indulge in sugar."

I held my breath, waiting to see what he thought of it. He chewed for what seemed like an eternity and swallowed, but didn't say anything right away. I couldn't hold it any longer. "Well?"

"They are quite good."

"Quite good? Seriously, that's all you have to say about the small piece of heaven you just ate?" I said, exasperated.

"You'll come to find that I don't give compliments easily or often. Take it or leave it."

This caused me to start laughing again. I should have known better than to expect him to react like a normal person would. "What else did you pack in your bag of tricks?"

"The normal things: a map, compass, satellite phone, Leatherman multitool, first aid kit, flashlight, binoculars, and food," Jay said, pulling out each item to show me.

"You have a satellite phone? Who has a satellite phone?" I said, snatching it out of his hands and looking it over.

"My dad owns one of the biggest private security companies in the eastern hemisphere. I work with him a lot and end up in places that phones don't work, like here," Jay explained.

"Wow! You do that and go to school? You must be crazy busy."

"I don't attend classes at Ryevick; I do online classes."

"Is that why I never see you on campus? I was wondering if you did all night classes or something."

"Yes, my father doesn't feel that Ryevick has much to offer me that he can't give me through experience. I have been working with him since I could shoot a gun."

I balked at that; I'd never been around guns, my family was very much against it. "How old was that?"

"I think it was about ten when I passed my qualifications, but I prefer a bow to a gun. Personally, I think it takes more skill to use than a gun."

"Holy shit, are you a ninja or something?"

Jay laughed and coughed, choking on his trail mix at that comment. "Is it because I'm Asian?"

"What? No, I mean you can shoot a gun and a bow, you run like the wind, and you snuck up on me like a ghost," I said, scowling at him.

He looked at me with contemplative eyes before he answered. "My father taught me to be a force to be reckoned with. I am skilled in many ways of fighting, infiltration tactics, and strategic planning."

"Remind me never to piss you off, but if I get in a tough spot, I'll know who to call," I said, bumping into him with my shoulder.

Jay stilled at my words; he turned to look at me, holding my gaze intently. "I know you're joking, but I truly hope that you know that I would come to your aid in an instant."

Under his intense gaze, I felt a trickle of fear at his words. It was the first time I truly got a glimpse of the person under the stoic expression. It would be terrifying if you found yourself his enemy. I hadn't a clue what caused Jay to consider me a friend, but I was thankful for it, knowing how dangerous he could be.

"Here, eat this; we still have to make it back to the car," Jay said, his mask back in place, handing me an energy bar.

"How far is it back to the car?" I asked, letting the topic change.

"About thirty minutes, but it's the toughest part of the trail."

"I should have known, by how wild the path was. How did you find this place anyway?"

"I like to go camping when things get crazy back at the house. It's more peaceful out here in the woods when Micah and Parker get into it."

"They're that bad, huh?"

Jay shook his head, "It's like two wild dogs fighting over the same bone. It's messy and loud, even Beth can't break them up sometimes."

"Who's Beth?" I asked, feeling irritated to hear a woman's name.

"She's the one who looks after us while we're here at school. Come on, let's get going."

I was already groaning as I stood, feeling my legs crying out to rest just a little longer. Jay wasn't kidding that the way back was rough. It was uphill the whole time, and the path was rocky with lots of shifting dirt to manage. When we reached the Jeep, I almost couldn't pull myself back into the seat, Jay had to give me a boost.

"Please tell me we aren't going to be doing this the rest of the week, I don't think I could survive that."

"No. I only go trail running once or twice a week. The track we did today I normally can only manage once a week, it's the hardest one I do."

"What the fuck, Jay! You took a beginner on a trail you can only manage to do once a week?"

"I told you I would challenge you. If I had told you, then you would never even have tried. Now look, you managed to do the whole thing. You're stronger than you give yourself credit for," Jay said looking at me out of the corner of his eye as he drove.

I stuck my tongue out at him and huddled in the seat, not looking at him but smiling to myself. I'd managed to do something like this on the first try. I should get a gold star and another cookie for that.

Nineteen

Lailah

The next two weeks flew by, and I fell into a routine that made me feel like I'd been living here on campus for much longer than two and a half months. Jay and I went running every morning, hitting the harder trails on the weekends. I could feel my strength and endurance get back to what it was when I was on the track team. With Jay pushing me to be better and to run faster, I was now able to beat him in some of our friendly races.

Hudson and I spent Tuesdays in the library study room, trying to improve my failing grade. I was excited because it was actually making sense, and I didn't feel quite so stupid. That is until I went to work with him in his lab on Thursdays. The math and material he was working with was like an alien language to me. He had me help mainly as his runner, grabbing slides, chemicals, and other equipment he needed. It was cool to see him in action and to spend time talking to him about what he was passionate about.

Brayden offered me a spot on the Halloween party organizers committee. We all helped to make the decorations, paint backgrounds for photo booths, and make sure we had everything we needed to make this one epic party. Parker popped up here and there, typically when Cami was busy or was spending quality time with Maggs. I think she felt bad that she was leaving me alone, so she sent him to keep me entertained.

Out of the five, the only one I didn't see much of was Micah. Not that I was looking to spend a whole lot of time with him, it just seemed odd he was never around much on campus. I had expected that me spending time with his best friend would mean he might be around more. Maybe it was more of a girl thing to include all your friends in everything.

I set my dinner tray down at the table Cami and I always sat at. She was doing dinner with her sisters, so I was on my own. Parker had texted me, telling me he was busy tonight too, with lots of sad crying emojis to show how he felt about me eating alone. It didn't bother me; I was used to being on my own. It wasn't until I met all of them that I was constantly surrounded by people.

A shadow crossed over the book I was reading, causing me to look up. Standing in front of me were four girls I recognized from my dorm. I groaned internally, knowing that this was not going to be enjoyable.

"Lailah, right?" one girl asked.

"Unfortunately," I muttered.

"We would like to have a word with you," another said.

I closed the book and heaved a big sigh. "How can I help you?"

"Is it true that you're going with all The Manor boys to the Halloween party?"

"I am attending the party, but I was only asked by Brayden," I said, trying to keep my answers simple so they couldn't read into it.

"Then why are Parker and Hudson telling girls they're going with you if you already have a date?"

"I can't control what they say or who they hang out with. I did not ask to go with them, and they didn't ask me. It looks like they might just be saying that, so they don't have to go with you guys." As soon as I said it, I knew it was the wrong thing to do, but I was so sick and tired of these girls causing trouble that it just slipped out.

One girl picked up my glass full of soda and tossed it in my face. I shut my eyes waiting for the cold, sticky liquid to hit me, but it never came. I felt my chair getting pulled away from the table, and someone stand in front of me. The girls all gasped. When I opened my eyes, I found Micah, of all people, blocking my view of them. He reached a hand up and wiped his face off with napkins someone handed to him.

"Oh my God, Micah, I'm so sorry. I seem to be so spacey today, I can't believe I spilled my drink like that," one girl said, her voice shaking.

I peered from behind him to look at their faces. Sure enough, they were scared shitless of Micah right now, and I couldn't be more pleased it was them and not me for a change.

"I think you had better go before your clumsy ass spills something else on me," Micah growled.

And just like that, they scattered like mice getting chased by a cat. Micah pulled out the chair next to me and sat down muttering as he tried to dry his shirt. I stared at him with bold curiosity. *Why had he just done that? What was he doing sitting next to me? Did he want something?*

"I'm not an animal in a zoo. It's rude to stare, or didn't your mother teach you that?" Micah said, meeting my gaze.

"Thank you," I said, not backing down from his challenging look.

"Whatever."

"How long were you watching?"

"Long enough to see you do a great impersonation of a doormat. Why didn't you do anything about it, you were just going to let them douse you because they're petty bitches?"

"I didn't ask for your help, and I certainly didn't ask for your advice," I snapped.

I wasn't sure what it was about Micah, but he seemed to set me off. I couldn't manage to keep him from getting under my skin.

"It's not advice, anyone with eyes could see that something was going to happen. It was almost too painful to watch, like some National Geographic shit where the lion takes out the gazelle."

"I'm confused. You come over here, take a bath in my soda for me, and now you're mad at me for not doing anything about it? Who the hell do you think you are?" I stood up from my seat, grabbed my book, and turned on my heel. Then on second thought, I turned and looked over my shoulder. "You want me to do something, well here is me walking away from an arrogant asshole who doesn't deserve my thanks."

I was so mad at him, I was shaking as I left the cafeteria. What really made me mad was the fact that as I was telling him off, he had excitement in his eyes, like he was proud of me for standing up to him.

"Fuck him," I said a little louder than I had intended.

"Lailah?"

I gulped as I turned slowly. "Hey, Brayden."

Great, I was just insulting his best friend right in front of him. Not good.

"You okay? Did someone do something?" he asked, reaching out and touching my arm.

A jolt of energy shot through me at his touch, just like it had with Jay on our first running hike. This time Brayden reacted, jerking his hand away from me and shaking it out like it stung.

"What was that?" I asked.

Brayden just shook his head, looking as confused as I felt. "I have no idea."

"Hey, dipshit, good thing you didn't get very far. You left your backpack behind," Micah said, walking up to us.

I snatched my bag from him, but our hands brushed, sending another electric current through my body.

"What the hell is that?!" I demanded as my backpack fell to the ground. "Why do I keep getting shocked when I touch people?"

"Wait, this happens to anyone you touch?" Brayden asked.

I shook my head, wrapping my arms around myself. "I don't know, maybe not everyone, but it happened with Jay a few weeks ago. Now it just happened twice with you guys."

"Lailah, I'm going to try and touch your arm again to see if it happens again," Brayden said as he slowly reached out. When his hand grasped my arm, nothing happened. "Did you feel anything?"

"No, nothing," I said. "I have no idea why it happens or when it chooses to do it. Is there something wrong with me?"

"No, nothing's wrong with you," Brayden said, pulling me into a hug.

I nestled into his chest, letting him hold me. I breathed in his soft scent that reminded me of fresh-turned earth and spring showers. He rubbed my back, helping to calm me down from my panic attack, making me feel more grounded. The comfort I felt in his arms was amazing, and like nothing I had ever experienced before.

"Hey, what happened?" I heard Parker's voice from behind me. "You say something mean to her, asshole?"

I could only assume he was talking to Micah. He wasn't wrong, but Micah wasn't the reason I was burrowed in Brayden's arms. I pulled away from him, not willing to let Micah get yelled at for something he didn't do.

"Parker, it wasn't him," I said, reaching to stop him from going after Micah.

"Wait, Lailah," Brayden said, trying to grab for me.

When I grabbed onto Parker's arm, instead of a spark like the other two, a jolt of power almost knocked me off my feet. I gasped as my hand locked around his arm, unable to let go.

"Fuck, Lailah, what's happening?" Parker looked at me with a worried expression.

I tried to let go, but no matter how I demanded that my hand release its hold, it wouldn't listen to me. Brayden came up behind me and placed his hand on my shoulders and started to knead his thumbs into my shoulder blades.

"Take a deep breath, Lailah. You need to calm down, breathe in through the mouth, out through the nose," he said calmly, resting his head against mine, so he didn't have to talk very loud. "That's a girl, nice easy breaths."

I tried to follow Brayden's direction and breathe the way he wanted, but the shuddering breaths came and went as they pleased. It was more the feel of him and his touch that seemed to calm me down. I relaxed into him, and once I was able to do that, the strange energy flowing through me stopped, and I could let go of Parker's arm. Brayden pulled me back to him, and he wrapped his arms and body around me, trying to get as much contact as he could. He kept talking to me in a calming voice, relaxing me further. Finally, I let go and closed my eyes, drifting into darkness.

Twenty

Micah

“What the hell did you do to her, Brayden?” Parker asked as he watched Brayden gather Lailah into his arms.

“She needed to be grounded, or her powers were going to explode right here in the middle of the quad. I might have overdone it a bit, but I’ve never done something like that before,” Brayden said, frowning at Parker.

“Well, if you’re concerned about people seeing something weird going on, you might want to go somewhere less obvious,” I said, looking at the students who were whispering to each other and looking at Brayden, who was holding a passed-out woman in his arms.

“Right. Well, if you don’t mind grabbing her backpack, we shouldn’t be lingering here,” Brayden said as he walked toward her dorm.

I shook my head, grabbed the bag she'd dropped, and slung it over my shoulder. We made quite the sight, Brayden holding Lailah, and Parker and I trailing after them.

"I thought you had an obligation tonight, which is why I was babysitting her," I grouched at Parker.

"It seems that my father didn't need me at the board meeting after all," Parker said as anger flashed in his eyes.

I grunted, not really caring to know the cause of that anger. I was more worried about the fact that Lailah had almost lost her control, and with her powers released, she could have taken the school out. The demon threat was getting worse, which is why we were all hanging around her all the time, but that was also making it worse. The more we interacted with her, the more the pull to Bond was building.

"Why are you wet?" Parker asked, giving me the side-eye.

I looked down, forgetting the fact that my shirt was still covered in soda. "I was protecting Lailah from The Manor boys' fan club. They were giving her a hard time about you all, saying you're going to the Halloween party with Lailah and no one else." I looked up at Parker's stupid, grinning face and glared at him. "Douche move to make her an even bigger target. You're the one that's her friend, and I don't have time to deal with bitch fights. So, if this is going to be a regular thing, I'm not babysitting anymore."

"You say that, but you're always lurking in the background, watching her. Don't think I haven't noticed you in the shadows like a stalker," Parker said. I tripped over my own feet, surprised that he would even notice.

Whenever the guys were with Lailah, they seemed to only have eyes for her. I felt the draw to be with her just as much as they did, but I knew that wasn't real. The angels made her that way so we would feel the need to Bond with her. Well, I wasn't falling for it. I didn't need anyone to worry about but myself. With her powers building, having more of us close to her wasn't helpful. Today was a perfect example. She would have been fine if Parker hadn't walked up, adding to the clusterfuck.

Three out of five was way too much energy to have around her at this point. If we had any hope of bringing her in before she exploded, we needed to move fast.

"Would one of you be so kind as to get the door for me? I seem to have my hands full," Brayden called out when we reached the door to the dorms.

"Fuck, sorry," Parker said, grabbing the door.

We headed for the elevator and stopped, looking at each other.

"Anyone know where her room is?" I huffed.

"You don't know?" Brayden asked Parker.

"Why the hell would I know where her room is?" he asked, offended.

Brayden shrugged. "Just assumed, since you hang out with her and Cami, you might have hung out here."

"Nope. She's never offered to have any of us to step foot in the dorm. We always meet out front," Parker said." Hold on, I'll call Cami."

"Don't tell her what happened, she's with Beth and Nona," Brayden warned.

"Shit, then I shouldn't call her. Beth has a sixth sense about shit like this," Parker said, putting his phone away.

I pulled out my phone and dialed the one person I knew would know.

"What, I'm busy."

"Jay, what's Lailah's room number?"

"Why do you need to know?"

"Look, she had a power flair and passed out. Cami is with Beth, and we need to get her to her room," I snapped, not seeing why I had to go into all the details.

"Tenth floor, room eight."

"Thanks," I said and hung up heading for the elevator. I hit the button for the tenth floor once we were in.

"How did you know Jay would know where her room was?" Parker asked.

I gave Parker a look, wondering if he was really this stupid. "It's Jay. Once he met her on the run and had her phone number, he did a full background check on her. Of course, he knows her room number, he would never let something like that go unknown."

"Why the fuck would he do that?" Parker asked.

I groaned, rolling my head back to stare at the ceiling of the elevator. "He talked to her, gave her Hudson's phone number, even had her program her number into his phone. Jay doesn't do things like that. So, you bet your ass he would do everything he could to find out who she is and why he did those things."

"Jay doesn't do friends," Brayden said, backing me up.

"Hmm, guess I've never seen him hang out with anyone but us and the guys he works with on jobs for his dad. Never thought about the fact he didn't have any other friends."

"God, you're as smart as a box of rocks. How are you one of the top ten smartest people with technology?" I said, stepping out of the elevator looking for room eight.

I started going through her backpack to find out where she would keep her keycard, but I couldn't find it. Then I looked at her in Brayden's arms, blonde hair cascading down like a golden waterfall. She nuzzled closer to Brayden's throat and sighed. She looked so fragile, and I hated it.

"I'm going to need to slip her key card out of her back pocket since it's not in her backpack," I said. Brayden adjusted his hold on her so it would be easier for me to get her key card without groping her.

"Oh, like hell you're reaching into her pants," Parker said, blocking me from reaching out to her.

"Because she would like the idea of you touching her ass better? I don't think she would appreciate any of us doing this," I pointed out.

"If anyone is going to do it, Brayden should. She doesn't seem to have a problem with him touching her," Parker said, making a good point. "Give her to me, Brayden."

"Okay." Brayden handed her over without jostling her too much.

She fidgeted in his arms but settled once she was cuddled against his chest, her hand clutching his shirt. Brayden made quick work grabbing her keycard and let us in. Her room was simple but homey. Family photos and letters were pinned on a corkboard by her desk. A soft-looking blanket covered in elephants was tossed over the back of her couch. I then noticed her bed had bright tie-dyed sheets on it with a well-loved stuffed elephant sitting by the pillow. *God, this chick is strange. Who picks elephants as a favorite animal?* I pulled back the sheet and noticed a book peeking out from under her pillow. I pulled it out and set it on the nightstand, so she didn't sleep on it. Parker set her down gently and pulled the covers over.

"Should we stay?" Brayden asked.

I shook my head. "Fuck no, she'd freak out if she woke up to us being in her room. If she hasn't invited any of you up before, I'm thinking this would not be a welcome way for that to happen."

"Well, what do you know," Parker said with his damn grin on display. "You do have a heart, though not enough for me to control it."

"Can it, dickweed," I said, heading out of the room and looked back when they didn't follow. "Let's go assholes, we don't need to set her off again. We are on the tenth fucking floor. I'm not getting blamed for the shit storm if she takes the building down."

We made our way back to the house in silence, unsure of what to do about Lailah. Brayden already texted Beth to tell her we, including Cami, needed to talk. Each of us needed to be on the same page, and Cami was one of the few people who wouldn't set off Lailah's powers by being around her. When we walked into the library, we found everyone waiting for us.

"What happened?" Beth said, walking over to us with worry showing in her eyes.

I first met Beth a week after my powers manifested. We all came together as kids during the summer—their master plan to get us to become a unit. Beth was our den mother, she broke up fights, bandaged us up, and made sure we ate our meals. She'd always been looking out for us, and it seemed that even though Lailah hadn't met her, Beth already considered her one of her cubs.

"Lailah's powers are at the breaking point. I'm not sure how much longer it will be before something triggers her coming into her element," Brayden said.

Beth turned to Jay. "I thought you said the running was helping to bleed off the extra energy?"

"She's growing stronger every day. I didn't account for the fact that she would advance so fast. None of us adapted as fast as she is. I've had to make the runs longer, harder, faster to get her to the point of being maxed out," Jay said. His face was neutral, but I could hear the irritation in his voice. He didn't like to be surprised and unsure of how to handle a problem.

"Like I've been saying, we need to leave her the hell alone. Yet these assholes are creating more problems by being attached to her all the time," I said, cocking a hip to lean on the back of one of the couches.

"What other problems?" Hudson asked.

He had been working with Nona to research all we knew about Synergy's powers, and from what I heard, it was very little.

"The fangirls are getting more aggressive toward her," I said, glaring at Parker. "The sprinklers the other week, I have to admit, was kind of brilliant. They're sure coming up with interesting ways to keep you guys from hanging out with her."

"Like you fucking care, you would just love it if we all walked away from her. It would be so much easier for you if we just ignored the fact that Synergy was here at school," Parker growled.

I could feel my blood begin to boil at his words. He didn't get it at all. How dare he assume to know how I was feeling? None of them understood what it meant to lose people they loved and cared about. How could they possibly understand that letting Lailah into our lives could be the end of everything?

"That's quite enough, Parker. Can we please stay on topic?" Beth said, frowning at us both. "I would have agreed that we need to back off, but with the increase of demon activity, we can't leave her vulnerable. It seems that bringing her into the fold sooner rather than later would be the best course."

"Can we wait till next week?" Brayden asked. "Just till after the Halloween party. I would like to let her have one last normal college experience before we destroy her whole world."

Beth contemplated that, tapping her finger on her chin. I wanted to tell Brayden that he was being a hopeless romantic, but I also saw his point. When she was told about what she really was, it would change her life forever. As much as I hated the idea of being bound to her forever, I didn't want her to hurt when the life she knew crumbled around her. I experienced that when my parents died, and I wouldn't wish that on anyone. Although I have to admit, seeing her get pissed at me when I pushed her buttons gave me hope that she wouldn't be a complete lamb to the slaughter.

"If you think she can make it to the end of the week without further incident, I will agree to wait. With one condition, though. You all need to make yourselves scarce for the rest of the week. We need to keep her under control until we can get her somewhere safe for her to experience her full power," Beth said, looking each one of us in the eye.

"Not a problem for me," I said. Parker rolled his eyes at me, and I flipped him off.

"I already needed to cancel with Lailah for our Thursday session, so I will just add on tomorrow's as well," Hudson said.

"My dad has been wanting me to take a job that will take me out of town till Thursday night, but she still needs to go running. Cami, can you make that happen?" Jay asked.

"God, please tell me you're not asking me to go running with her? I fucking hate running. What else could we do to help burn off the extra energy?" Cami asked.

"Sex would be an acceptable alternative," Jay said with a blank face.

Cami choked on her own spit at that answer. "Excuse me?"

"There is no way in hell that I'm going to allow that to happen," Parker said, storming up to Jay. "Come up with something else."

"He does make a good point, although research says oral sex uses more energy than standard intercourse. The most energy burned though is actually a make-out session lasting thirty minutes or more," Hudson said, stunning us all into silence.

"I would hope you're joking, Hudson, but I've known you long enough to know that you're not," Brayden said, eyes wide with shock.

I groaned as I pictured Lailah's perfect mouth going down on me, and her crystal-blue eyes looking up at me as I fisted a handful of her hair. Just because I didn't want to be stuck with her for life didn't mean I was blind. She was hot. My body temperature began to rise as my heartbeat gained speed. If I didn't get those damn innocent eyes out of my mind, I was literally going to combust.

"God damn you, Hudson," I snarled and stormed out of the room, needing to calm myself down.

I heard someone follow after me and was surprised to find that it was Cami, and not Brayden, who grabbed my arm.

"What do you want, ankle biter?" I said, jerking my arm from her grasp.

Cami put her hands on her hips and looked up at me. "Look, cockwaffle, I get that you might not love the idea of Synergy being a human, but you're the only one of the guys who hasn't even given her a chance. Lala is one kick-ass chick who will surprise you if you just took a second to know her."

"I don't need to give her a chance or get to know her. She's only here to get us to bond to her so she can take over our powers and use us as she sees fit," I said, disgusted at the idea. "You don't have to worry about what she'll do to you because you're completely human. You don't have fire shooting out of your hands, setting things on fire when you can't control it. You didn't have to spend five years training your ass off to learn to bend your powers to your will. I'm one of the only fire Elementi who hasn't killed one of their instructors by accident. I can't allow someone else to fuck this up for me no matter how *kick-ass* a chick she is."

This time when I stormed off, she didn't stop me, but I could feel the pity in her eyes, like lasers drilling into my back. I couldn't let Lailah get under my skin, and the best way to do that was to keep the hell away from her.

Twenty-One

Lailah

I opened my eyes to find that I was in complete darkness. It wasn't the kind of darkness that had a soft edge to it. No, this was void of any light to give me a hint of where I was. I felt my panic begin to rise as I stood up carefully. I couldn't remember how I ended up in this place, wherever it was. I took a small tentative step forward, reaching my hands out in front of me as far as I could, trying to feel for anything familiar around me. I made my way forward with my heartbeat banging in my chest and my ears straining to hear anything that would give me some clue as to what was going on. The only thing I could make out was my ragged breathing as it was eaten up by the silence. I started to shake, my fear seeping into my bones with the realization that I could die here, and no one would know. No one would find me until it was too late. That fear crept up my spine like cold fingers, making me flinch from its touch.

"Please let someone find me, anyone. Oh God, please don't let me die here," I whispered.

Out of the darkness, I felt a presence, one that made me want to curl up into a ball and hide. I knew whatever was out there was going to kill me, and I couldn't do a thing about it. I was defenseless against this evil that was inching closer to me. I gasped, trying to breathe while my lungs refused to fill with air from the fear choking me. Tears started to stream down my cheeks as the knowledge of my fate settled in the pit of my stomach.

"I taste your fear, and it's like fine wine on my tongue," a raspy voice said, cutting through the silence. "How foolish of them to leave you so vulnerable and ripe for the taking."

The voice was like nails on a chalkboard, grating and sending my body into convulsions. I fought to stay on my feet, unwilling to let this creature take more from me.

"Look how the little lamb fights against the inevitable, such spirit. Too bad we'll never get to see what you would have become once unleashed on the world," the voice said, sounding much closer than it was before. "My master will be so pleased to know we took you from the world before the angel's little warriors got their new weapon."

I fought back a scream when I felt a sharp claw caress my cheek. My body shook with the terror coursing through it. I tried to fight against the hold my panic had on me. I needed to think of something to save myself. How could I just stand here knowing it was going to kill me without a drop of care or guilt afterward? Spinning on my heel, I ran away from the evil energy as fast as I could. I pushed myself hard, knowing that my life depended on getting away from this *thing* that was trying to kill me.

"The little lamb can run. But for how long?" the voice laughed, sending pinpricks of pain all over my body.

Ignoring the taunt, I ran. Jay had been pushing me hard the past few weeks, and I knew I couldn't keep this speed up forever, but I could do it long enough to come up with a better plan. Wracking my brain, I kept trying to figure out some way that I could get out of this alive. The only problem was that I didn't know what I was dealing with. Was I dreaming? Was I trapped in a building? Was I still at the school? Had I been kidnapped? Why the fuck was this happening, and what the hell was this creepy fuck talking about?

My thoughts drifted back to Jay and the conversation we'd had at the waterfall. He'd promised to come help me whenever I needed it, no matter what he was doing. I checked my pockets to see if, by chance, they had forgotten about my cell, but I wasn't so lucky. I kept my legs pumping, keeping the distance between the psycho killer and me. I cried out as I took a misstep and twisted my ankle, crashing to the floor.

"No, no, no, no; this can't be happening," I said, trying to get back on my feet, but I crashed back to the floor when my ankle gave out.

I started to crawl, anything to keep me moving forward. I wept as I called out for Jay, begging with everything I had that he would be able to find me and save me. A warm breeze stirred in the darkness, wrapping me with its comfort. It felt like being surrounded by the waterfall's mist. I sobbed, knowing deep in my soul that Jay had heard me and was coming to help me. A flare of blinding light surrounded me; I covered my eyes, seeing stars from the sudden shock of light. I blinked as fast as I could to clear my vision. When I looked up, I found Micah standing in front of me. His eyes flashed with a fury that I'd never seen in anyone before. At first, I thought he was pissed at me for something, but then he scooped me up, and I knew I was safe.

I clung to him, and the heat from his body seeped into me, chasing away the rest of the fear that had been clinging to me. Brayden stepped up on his right, followed by Parker. On Micah's left, Jay materialized with Hudson next to him. They all looked ready to kill, bodies rigid with anger. I looked forward and saw a shifting apparition of black smoke on the edge of the light that was emanating from Micah.

"Begone demon, you are not welcome here. She is under our protection, and you will not touch one hair on her head," Micah declared, his voice vibrating through his chest.

The shadow hissed. "My master won't lose to the likes of you, even if you have your sixth. We will come for her again, and the next time, you won't be so lucky."

"Luck has nothing to do with it. We are her protectors to call, and we will always answer," Brayden said, stepping forward, closer to me.

"The lamb will die before you can truly take that role, Elementi. You are not as safe as you think you are," the demon said before he vanished into the darkness.

I clung to Micah and cried. I let the tears stream down my face as he just stood there, holding me tightly to him. I felt the others come around me, someone touched my shoulder, someone else stroked the top of my head, then someone else's hand wrapped around my ankle, followed by another hand on my calf. I felt their energy hum along my skin, filling me with comfort and assurance. My tears slowed, then stopped, and I relaxed, being held and cared for by them. The rightness of it all settled my soul, making me feel more complete than I ever had in my life.

"It's time to wake up now," Brayden said, whispering in my ear, then placing a gentle kiss on my cheek.

With those words, my eyes flew open, and I found myself in my dorm room. I laid there, taking a few deep breaths to calm my heart rate before making my next move. I sat up slowly and looked around my room, noticing Cami, who was sleeping on the couch, wrapped in my elephant blanket. I slipped out of my bed and stood up carefully, not really believing that my ankle could be okay. There was no pain or sign that I'd done anything to hurt myself. Silently, I walked over to Cami, sat on the coffee table next to the couch, and shook her awake gently.

"Cami," I said gently. "Hey, wake up. I need to talk to you."

Cami grumbled and pulled the blanket over her head. I looked over at my nightstand and saw that it was three in the morning. I shook her harder this time, pulling the blanket off of her.

"Cami!"

This time she shot up, looking around bleary-eyed till she focused on me. "Lala, what's wrong?" She slid her feet to the floor, so she was sitting, looking at me and rubbing her eyes clear of sleep.

"Why are you in my room?" I asked, feeling like I'd missed something important.

"What do you remember about last night?" she countered.

I rubbed my forehead, trying to organize my thoughts. "I was eating dinner and some girls were giving me a hard time about the Halloween party. Micah was there too. We argued, and I left. After that, I don't really remember much. I think Parker and Brayden might have shown up at some point, then it all goes blank."

Cami took my hands in hers, drawing my attention back to her. "You passed out in the middle of the quad. We don't know why, but thankfully, Micah, Brayden, and Parker were close by. They brought you back to your dorm and waited until I could get back to look after you."

I frowned. "I passed out? That's so odd. I don't remember ever doing that before." I could feel a headache building with all this confusing information. "I also just had the worst nightmare of my life."

"Want to talk about it?" Cami asked, squeezing my hands.

I shook my head as I stood up. Walking over to my backpack, I pulled out some pain meds. "Not really, I just want to go back to sleep and hope to God that I don't dream again."

"Would a snuggle buddy help?" Cami asked as I swallowed the pills.

I smiled at her, glad that she was here and I didn't have to wake up alone. "Sure, I'll take whatever defense I can get."

I crawled back into bed, clutching Elle to my chest. Cami joined me, laying on her side, so I had her back and she faced the rest of the room. I let my head lean against her back, so I could hear her heartbeat. The steady rhythm lulled me to sleep faster than I thought it would happen. Thankfully, I didn't have any other nightmares and slept deeply.

"Lala, you gotta get up, or you're not gonna to have time to get ready for class," Cami said as she poked me gently.

I groaned, not wanting to leave my bed just yet. I rubbed the sleep from my eyes and looked up at her. "How are you awake before me?"

"It's ten o'clock, silly."

That had me sitting up and tossing the blankets off me. "What? How is it so late already? I never sleep that late. Oh God, I stood Jay up. I have to call him."

I hopped out of bed and started looking for my phone, but couldn't remember the last place I had put it. Cami stepped in front of me, holding out my phone, rolling her eyes at me for freaking out.

"I already texted Jay and told him you had a rough night and needed sleep. Besides, you passed out yesterday, your body must've been exhausted from everything you've been doing," Cami said as she gathered up her stuff. "Oh, he also said that he's going on a work trip and will be gone until the weekend."

I felt my shoulders sag at that. Running with Jay had become one of my favorite parts of my day. I knew I couldn't slack off and wait till he came back; he would expect me to still keep training to be able to keep up with him when he returned.

"What if you switched up your workout for the week?" Cami said.

"What did you have in mind?" I asked, surprised. I knew how much Cami hated to work out.

"There's a kickboxing class that I like to go to off campus if you want to join me. There's a class tonight if you feel up to it."

"I should have guessed that if you did work out, it would involve you hitting something. Check-in with me at dinner, and I'll let you know how I'm feeling."

"Works for me! See you later, Lala. Text me if you need anything," Cami said as she headed out so I could get ready.

I looked down at my watch, and I cursed, seeing I had just thirty minutes to get ready and make it to class. I threw on a random T-shirt and a pair of jeans and ran out the door with my backpack. I made it to my labs on time, but it took me a few minutes to calm down and concentrate. I could tell that the time I spent with Hudson was making a major change in my chem class. When the teacher was talking, I no longer felt as lost as I once did, and I followed along more confidently.

Thankfully, Tuesdays were easy days, and I made it through classes easily enough, though I'd skipped breakfast. Cami waved to me from our table in the cafe, I dropped my stuff off and headed to order some food along with my chai. As I was waiting for my muffin to be warmed, I felt my phone vibrate. Pulling it out of my pocket, I saw it was a text from Hudson.

Hudson: **Hey, I won't be able to meet up this week. If you have any questions feel free to reach out. I'll try and get back to you when I get the chance.**

I didn't respond right away, unsure of what to say to him. Going a week without his help would be a good test to see how I was really doing, but I was bummed. Working with Hudson in his lab was always a good time. We seemed to work well together, and I was always blown away by his intelligence. I took a deep breath and wrote out my response.

> Me: **Sure thing! Hope our teacher isn't working you too hard. Will I still see you this weekend?**

> Hudson: **Of course, I wouldn't miss going to the party.**

For some reason, his answer wasn't what I wanted him to say. He was still going to be at the party, and I was already going with Brayden, but I wanted to hang out with him, too. Before I could reply, Hudson sent another text a second later.

> Hudson: **I didn't forget my promise to show you that I can have fun once in a while.**

Unable to stop myself, I grinned at my phone with a warm feeling fluttering in my stomach. He hadn't forgotten the conversation we'd had when I found out he'd never gone to any kind of party. Well, after I told him birthday parties didn't count. Now that I had one college rager under my belt, it was time to share the love.

"Large chai latte with a pumpkin muffin!" the barista called out, sounding like she had called the order more than once. Shaking myself out of my daze, I grabbed my items and headed back to Cami.

"You okay? They called your order twice before you responded."

"Fine. I was just texting Hudson and got distracted," I said, breaking apart my muffin.

Cami's fingers darted out snatching a piece. "What's that nerdy wizard up too?"

I scowled at Cami for stealing my food and moved it out of her reach. "Get your own. He was just letting me know we wouldn't be meeting this week."

"Hmm," Cami said with a mouth full of muffin.

"Seems like my week is freeing up, just when I got into a routine," I said, munching on my muffin.

"Sounds like the perfect time to have a girls-only week. I know we've both been busy with things going on, but I would love to get a chance to hang with you and Maggs," Cami said, unable to look me in the eyes.

I felt my brows rise in surprise. "Are we at the point where you're going to finally admit that Maggs is your girlfriend?"

"Yeah, I guess you could say we made it Facebook official yesterday," Cami said, grinning at me.

I clapped my hands excitedly and slid my muffin back between us. "In celebration, you may share my muffin with me."

"*Oh-kay,* let's not make this a major thing, Lala."

"Why? It is a major thing! I am so excited for you, and now that I have more friends to hang out with, you don't have to worry about leaving me alone all the time."

"Fat chance. You can't get rid of me that easily. Just because I have a lady friend doesn't mean that we won't be best friends."

"I wasn't thinking that, Cami. I just know that you worry about me, and now you're going to have someone else to worry about besides me."

Cami laughed. "Trust me. One of the most attractive things about Maggs is that she can take care of herself just fine."

"Should have guessed that a damsel in distress wouldn't be your type."

"If you come to kickboxing tonight, you'll see just how well she can manage," Cami said, wagging her eyebrows suggestively.

"Alright, you talked me into it. I'll go with you."

"Awesome! I'll let Maggs know, and we'll head over around six-thirty."

"Works for me. I'm heading to the library to get some homework done before we go," I said, grabbing my backpack.

"That's my cue, see you later," Cami said, grabbing her coffee and heading out of the cafe.

Crossing the quad to the library, I found an open spot to camp out in for the next few hours. I popped on my headphones, selected my favorites playlist on my phone, and got down to business. I worked on the edits for the second draft of my English paper, totally absorbed, ignoring the world around me. Needing to reference something from my notebook, I bent down to grab it when someone ripped the headphones off my head and let them clatter to the ground. Jerking back up, anger swirling in me for being treated so rudely, I shouldn't have been surprised by who I saw standing in front of me.

Mallory. Of course, her posse was with her, ready to back her up. "We have some unfinished business with you."

I sighed; I'd never been very good at dealing with situations like this. I always ran from my problems rather than confronting them. The need to make friends and have people like me always turned me into a doormat. At some point over the past few months, something in me had changed. Maybe it was Cami's confident influence, or possibly the fact that I now had more friends than I'd ever had in my life, but I was getting tired of running from these girls.

"What do you want, Mallory?" I asked, closing my laptop.

Mallory glared down at me, hands on her hips like she was some kind of supervillain. "We want The Manor boys back. Ever since you became friends with them, they've been blowing every other girl off."

I shook my head and let out a heavy breath. "What makes you think I can control what they do? I don't force them to hang out with me over you and your crew."

"Listen, you little bitch, no one has ever been able to grab the attention of more than one of them. There is something you're not sharing with the rest of us that gives you some hold on them." Mallory bent at the waist, so we were now at eye level. "Either share your secret, or we will have to do something more . . . drastic."

I laughed in her face, unable to stop myself. I couldn't believe this was happening to me. Some of the most popular girls at school were threatened by little old me. This was a twist that I never saw coming in my wildest dreams.

"Let's say I tell you what I did to get them to like me. What would you do with that information? You don't seem like the type to share well with others," I said, my voice filled with my disdain.

Mallory looked at me with a glint in her eyes, telling me everything I needed to know. Once she had the information, she was going to use it as she saw fit. I could just see the guys like magic genies bending to her will, enslaved to her need to have what people wanted.

"You let me worry about that because once you tell me, they won't be any of your concern."

I leaned in, closing the small distance between us so I could whisper in her ear. "Make sure you're paying attention, Mallory, I'm only going to say this once."

I paused, feeling the tension in her body, desperate for what I was going to tell her. The power I held in the situation blazed through my veins. I knew, deep down in my soul, that the next words out of my mouth were the truth, even if I wasn't ready to act on it yet.

"They are mine," I hissed in her ear, causing her to rear back from me. "Trust me when I say I will never hand them over to a conniving cunt like you. Stay the fuck away from them, or *I* might have to do something drastic."

Lightning-fast, she whipped out with her hand and slapped me across the face so hard I knew my cheek glowed with her handprint. I closed my eyes and took a breath before I shot out of my seat and returned the favor, but I did it with a closed fist. The impact of my knuckles meeting her jaw hurt, but the terrified look on her face made it worth it.

"That's the last warning I'll give you, Mallory. Stay the hell away from me, and stay the fuck away from *my guys*." I swept up the rest of my stuff and headed out of the library before anyone could react.

Once outside, I wasn't sure if I was horrified at my action or wanted to jump for joy. I felt electric. I'd never stood up for myself like that. It was exhilarating and empowering, but once that faded, I realized what I'd done. *What the fuck did I just do? I had no right to claim those guys. Not only did I deck a girl for going after them, I declared to the whole school that they were mine. Oh God, they're going to hate me. I can't claim ownership of five guys. I'm not even romantically involved with any of them. Sure, Brayden and I went on a date, kind of, I think. Then it was crashed by Parker and Hudson. So, I'm not sure what that turned it into. A triple date? Ha! Who am I kidding? There is no way those guys could ever share a woman when they can't share the same room without arguing.*

I made it to the dorm, and I raced up to my room, dumped my stuff, then ran down to Cami's room. I knocked on the door and waited, tapping my foot and biting my thumbnail.

"Lala? I thought you were studying?" Cami said when she opened the door. She took a moment to look and then her face sobered. "What's wrong? What happened? Did someone *slap* you!?"

Cami grabbed my face with a hand to look at my cheek, then dragged me into her room. She sat me down on her couch, which was amazingly clear of clothes.

"Maggs, can you grab an ice pack from my fridge?" Cami asked.

It was then that I noticed Cami was only wearing a big T-shirt and nothing else. I felt my face flush with my embarrassment when I noticed Maggs slipping out of Cami's bed.

"Oh, God, Cami, I'm so sorry. I didn't mean to . . ."

"Shut up, Lala. Someone hit you, you did the right thing coming to me," Cami said, gently placing the icepack on my cheek. "Now, tell me what happened."

"You told me to shut up," I said, taking the pack from her and feeling the need to lighten the heavy mood in the room before I broke into tears.

Cami gave me a stern look I'd never seen from her before. She was taking this situation very seriously, and it was freaking me out more than I already was.

"Mallory happened," I said.

"Should have guessed that snooty bitch was the problem," Maggs said, sitting on my other side, placing a comforting hand on my shoulder.

"I was minding my own business when she and her girl gang cornered me and demanded a chat. She wanted me to tell her how I got all the guys to be interested in me and no one else. Not so subtly, she threatened me, and I got pissed off."

"I didn't know you could get pissed, Lala." Cami looked at me in surprise. "Sure, I've seen you get mad, but not something worth getting you slapped."

"Never been threatened before, I guess," I said, shrugging my shoulders. "I told her that they were mine, and she could fuck off."

Cami and Maggs stilled, shocked at my words, before Cami started laughing, and Maggs joined in. I couldn't help smiling at my response to Mallory's threat. It was totally out of character for me to say or do something like that.

"What I wouldn't give to have been there when you told her that," Maggs said, wiping her eyes with a finger. "I can see why she slapped you. She's not one who handles being told no very well."

"She's going to make your life hell, you know that, right?" Cami warned.

I shook my head. "I'm not so sure about that since I decked her in the face and threatened her before I left."

"You did what?" Cami gasped.

"God, Cami, I can see why you two are best friends. She's a little spitfire, all right," Maggs said, falling back onto the couch, laughing.

"When she slapped me, I lost it. I couldn't stop myself. I was so tired of them bothering me, and then she was threatening me to get her grubby hands on my guys. I couldn't help myself."

Cami shook her head and gave me an odd look like she knew something I didn't. "Your guys, huh?"

"You know what I mean," I snapped, not liking that she was focusing on that point.

Cami flopped against the couch, looking way too pleased with herself. "The guys are going to love this when they find out. Lord, the Halloween party is going to be so much better because of this."

I frowned, not understanding.

"Lala, I love you to bits, but how you manage through life I'll never understand," Cami teased. "You just told the whole school you're dating them—all of them."

Cami let that information hang in the air waiting for it to hit home for me. I groaned, letting the ice pack fall into my lap. "No one could really believe that could they?"

"Guess we're going to find out."

"So, are we still going to kickboxing?" Maggs asked, her eyes shining with humor. "Looks like you might need to hone your skills if you want to beat off all the unwanted girls from your guys."

I rolled my eyes but laughed with them at the image that played in my head. "Maybe they'll teach me to punch better, so next time my hand doesn't hurt so badly after."

Twenty-Two

Lailah

T he rest of the week passed without further incident, and the rumors I was afraid would be spreading didn't get much traction. Seems that no one believed I could date more than one guy at a time, so they dismissed it. The other reason might have been that the guys were busy all week, and I wasn't seen with them at all. Cami, Maggs, and I enjoyed the week doing fun girl stuff and taking self-defense classes as a joke. Cami kept telling me that I couldn't let someone get the drop on me like Mallory did. I had to be honest, the classes did make me feel better about protecting myself.

The day of the party had finally arrived, and I spent the whole morning decorating the large hall where the school held events. Now that I was covered in paint and sweat, and all the final touches were set up, I was heading back to the dorm to get ready for the fun to start. As I walked down the hall, I saw everyone running in and out of each other's rooms, giggling, chatting, and in various states of undress. Clothes and other items were getting tossed from one room to another as girls hollered from somewhere in their rooms. Dodging the chaos, I made it to the bathroom and managed to find an open shower to rinse off in.

I grabbed my stuff and headed down to Cami's room, where we had agreed to get ready. I had never been very big into Halloween since I didn't really have friends to do stuff with. I went with my little brother when he was younger, but that stopped four years ago. Cami flung her door open and pulled me inside the moment I knocked on her door.

"Let's see it. No more holding out on us," Cami said, her hands on her hips.

Cami and I had argued all week about what costume I was going to wear. I promised her I had something I could make work for the occasion.

"Um, I'm wearing it," I said, looking down at my clothes.

"Nope, no, hell no, there is no way that is going to fly. Maggs, I told you we couldn't trust her."

Maggs walked up, looking like the picture-perfect replica of a red-haired vintage barbie doll. Cami, on the other hand, was dressed like tomb raider, and I expected nothing less from her. Compared to them, my shirt that said *This is my costume.* was sadly lacking.

"This is what I have, so you're going to have to deal with it," I said, shrugging my shoulders.

"You really didn't think I would let you pick your own costume, did you? I got one for you weeks ago when I figured out that you were going to be terrible at this," Cami said, giving me a sly smile as she walked over to the couch where a dress bag was laying.

She unzipped it and revealed a dress that was a pale yellow and seemed to shine in the light. I walked over and touched the fabric, surprised to feel that it was a soft velvet. It looked like a replica of a medieval-style dress. It was simple in shape and didn't have a crazy amount of detail on it, and I was in love.

"Well? Are you going to put it on, or do I have to strip you myself?" Cami asked, grinning at me.

"Fine, you win," I said, tugging off my shirt and slipping the dress over my head.

I shimmied out of my jeans and let the dress fall around my legs. It fit snuggly to my chest and waist, but then it fell away loose and flowing. The sleeves were long and angled, so they almost brushed the floor. Cami walked over with a long string of pearls, wrapped it around my waist a few times, and let the rest drape down the front of the dress.

"How did you find something like this?" I said, twirling and looking at myself in Cami's full-length mirror.

"Surprisingly, no one here at school likes historically-based costumes, so it wasn't too difficult. It's not slutty enough for most of the girls," Maggs said as she sat me down and started doing something with my hair while Cami started to attack me with makeup.

"What's with all the effort, it's just a school party," I said. They were making me feel nervous.

"You want the first time you see all the guys since you claimed them for your harem lookin' like a bum?" Cami said.

"Seriously, Cami. I did not do that. How many times do we have to go over this? I don't even know if they all like me that way," I grumbled.

"As many times as it takes for you to get it through your head, that's what you did. Also, you're an idiot if you think they don't want you in that way. Lord, anyone with eyes can see the way they watch you."

"You make it sound so simple. We've never talked about crap like this. I wouldn't be surprised if they didn't talk to me at all tonight."

Cami laughed and booped me on the nose. "Lala, just you wait and see. They haven't been around you all week, so they will be running to your side the moment they see you."

I sat silently as they finished working on me. Once they were done, I got to look at myself. What I saw wasn't the same Lailah Mackenzie who showed up to school three months ago. This version of myself was much happier and sure of herself. I grinned at the woman in the mirror and turned to hug Cami and Maggs.

"Thanks, guys. This is amazing!"

"Any time, girlie," Maggs said, hugging me back.

"Come on, we're already late, as usual," Cami said, hugging me back, then took Maggs's hand as we headed out of the room.

As we walked over to the hall where the dance was taking place, it was fun to see everyone in their costumes. Some people got really creative, and others were so generic it made me shake my head. With the doors open to the cool night, the music could be heard before we even got close. The entrance was mobbed with people taking pictures with each other in the dying light. We managed to shove our way into the hall. People were already on the dance floor, grinding on one another. Most of the others were wandering around the border where we had the photo stations set up and props that went with each theme.

"Lailah, this looks amazing, you guys did a wonderful job!" Maggs said, giving me a side hug. "You'll have to help me with the next party we throw at my house."

"I'd love that," I said, nearly yelling over the noise.

"Oh, look, witch's brew. I gotta try that. Wonder if anyone's spiked it yet," Cami hollered as she dragged both of us after her.

It was cool to see the dry ice giving off the smoky effect that we'd hoped it would. The large cauldron was filled with green juice with gummy eyeballs floating around for added drama.

I helped myself to some, and the moment it hit my tongue, I knew it had been spiked with something strong.

"Hell yeah, this is going to be a great night!" Cami whooped as she chugged and refilled her cup.

"If you get shwasted tonight, I'm not babysitting you as you puke your guts out," Maggs warned Cami.

I smiled, the more time I spent with them, the more I knew that she was a perfect fit for Cami's wild side. Cami pouted at her but nodded her understanding. Something caught her eye, and she grinned, elbowing me. "Looks like one of them found you."

I turned in the direction she was looking, and my jaw hit the floor. Hudson was making his way over to us, and I prayed that it would take him a minute so I could stare at him longer. He had on tight-fitting black pants with a long elegant jacket that fit him so snuggly I was afraid it would rip. It had blue waves embroidered on the edge of the cuffs and halfway up the sleeve. The embroidery was along the bottom of the jacket as well. The deep-blue shirt under the jacket set the whole thing off. I had to check to make sure I wasn't drooling before he reached me.

"Lailah, you look amazing," he said, leaning close to my ear so I could hear him.

I felt his hand brush against my hip as he pulled back to look me in the eye. I placed a hand on his chest to balance as I leaned into him and found his shirt was silky against my touch. "You look quite dashing yourself."

We grinned at each other while I kept my hand on his chest, not willing to give up his closeness after a week without it. Another hand brushed down my back, drawing my attention, and I found Parker standing behind me. I had been so focused on Hudson that I hadn't noticed him. Parker was dressed as a pirate with a billowing purple shirt that was only buttoned halfway up. I grinned at him and wrapped my arms around his waist, hugging him tightly.

"Hey, Trouble, you miss me?" he asked, chuckling into my hair as he hugged me back.

"I guess you could say that. It's been a rather boring week without you guys," I said, returning his grin.

"That's not what I heard. Did you really deck Mallory?" he asked.

"Hell yeah I did, that bitch slapped me."

Parker laughed and hugged me tightly to him again before letting me go.

"Do I get a hug?" Brayden asked, sidling up beside me wrapping his arm around my hips, tugging me from Parker.

"Since you asked," I said, allowing him to pull me into his arms.

He held me tight and placed a gentle kiss on my head before letting me go. Finally getting to take in his costume, he looked like the Count of Monte Cristo. His Victorian jacket had an intricately woven tree embroidered on the back in greens and browns.

"You guys look so dashing," I said, not sure who to stare at first.

Then I caught sight of Micah and Jay walking over to our group. I gulped at the sight of the black T-shirt poured onto Jay's chest. I could see the outline of all the muscles I knew were under there. He paired it with a pair of black and white military camo pants and black boots. He looked more ready to kill than to party, but I was just glad he was here. Micah had on a bright-red shirt covered with a leather jacket that had flames crawling up it. He looked like the leader of some motorcycle gang, and it was totally working for me.

"Looks like the gang's all here," Cami yelled at me. "We're going to do our own thing since it seems like you're going to be busy." With a wink, she was gone, leaving me with the best eye candy our school had to offer.

I wasn't sure if it was the fact that we had spent time away, but feeling them close to me seemed to settle me in a way I didn't know I was missing. They had become such a huge part of my life in such a short time. It scared me as much as I loved it.

"So, are we going to stand here all night staring at each other or what?" Parker said, making everyone glare at him. "What? This is a party, right? Let's party!"

Without warning, Hudson surprised me by grabbing my wrist and pulling me onto the dance floor with the ever-growing mass of bodies. He shoved his way through the crowd, causing people to swear at him until they saw who it was, and then they moved out of his way with apologies. Once we got to a spot that seemed to work for him, he let go of my hand and started to sway to the music. I was nervous, since I'd only ever danced once before, and I'd been drunk at the time. Hudson, much to my amazement, was very comfortable on the dance floor. They always said that it was the quiet ones you needed to watch out for. A new song started that moved a little faster than the last one, and I was caught off guard when he stepped into my space, causing me to step back.

"Trust me," he said as he gently put his hands on my hips and guided me in how he wanted me to move. Once I figured out what he was trying to get from me, I relaxed to the rhythm of the song. I was so caught up that I didn't realize that Parker had come up behind me and was following along with our movements.

This reminded me of the dream I'd had some weeks ago, but that was Brayden and Parker on the dance floor, not Hudson. I was about to bolt from the dance floor, when the song changed to something slower. Hudson backed off, and Parker wrapped his arms around me and pulled me close. Of all the guys, I was strangely comfortable with Parker manhandling me. This, however, sent my libido into overdrive. I was covered from head to toe, but I still felt like this dress didn't give me much coverage.

"You've gotten better at this, Trouble," Parker whispered along my neck.

I shivered at his touch and fought against everything in me to turn in his arms. I wasn't willing to make a move on any of them until we had talked about things between us. If they knew about Mallory, then they knew about what I'd said. I couldn't let something as big as this be a misunderstanding. I allowed myself to relax in his hold and let him guide my body how he wished. I closed my eyes, enjoying the contact when someone was shoved into me. My eyes flew open as I felt a bone-chilling cold fill my body. I was suddenly scared, my heart racing as I looked around to see who had run into us. With everyone in costume, I couldn't tell who anyone was at a glance. I pulled out of Parker's arms and looked around.

"What's wrong?" Parker asked, grabbing my arm to stop me from running off.

"Nothing, I just need some air, there are too many people," I said, needing to get out of the crowd.

I don't know who or what I'd come into contact with, but I knew I didn't want it to happen again. This many people packed into a small space was just too unnerving for me right now. Parker took my hand and led me off the dance floor to an area where we had set up tables. I pulled on his arm and shook my head, pointing to the door, so we could head outside. I needed to hear myself think, and the music was way too loud. Smiling, he changed his direction and led us outside where I took a deep calming breath.

"Hey, everything okay?" Brayden asked, jogging up to us.

"Yeah, I just got overwhelmed with so many people," I said, sitting on a bench off to the side.

A short while later, Hudson joined us with drinks for everyone. Thankfully, it was just water, and none of that spiked punch. "You looked like you needed some hydration."

I smiled at him. "Thanks for looking out."

Gulping down the water helped to even out my adrenaline. Something about that cold feeling had me remembering that awful nightmare I had earlier that week. I shivered, thinking of that darkness that made me want to give up in defeat. Turning to set the empty cup down beside me, I jumped as

I noticed that Jay was sitting there, watching me with his dark, unreadable eyes.

"You really need to stop trying to give me a heart attack, Jay," I said, glowering at him.

Jay smirked at me. "You just need to get better at reading your surroundings."

"Leave it to you to turn this into a training session."

"Speaking of which, did you keep up with your running?"

I shook my head but grinned knowingly. "I decided to try something else. Cami and I did a bunch of kickboxing and self-defense classes."

"Good." He nodded. "Building your strength is smart since you have good stamina."

"I'm glad you approve. We'll have to test out my skills one of these days. I seem to remember you telling me you know quite a few fighting styles," I said, smiling at him.

Jay returned my smile with his own version. "That could be interesting."

I looked up to see all the guys were milling about, watching over me while I pulled myself together. "You guys don't need to wait on me. Go, have fun, enjoy the party."

"Nah, I'm good hanging out with you," Parker said, plopping down on my other side. "Besides, I heard somewhere around school that no females were allowed to hang around us, or they would get punched by a certain someone."

I blushed and ducked my head, so I didn't have to look at them. "Yeah, sorry about that. It came out in the heat of the moment."

"I should be thanking you. Ever since that happened, the vultures stopped circling," Micah said.

My head shot up, hearing Micah's response. I wanted to gape at him but didn't want to let on how surprised I was in case he was just pulling my leg.

"Man, I can't believe you really did it. I saw her the next day, and her jaw was all swollen and black-and-blue," Hudson said, rubbing his own jaw.

"Growing up with brothers was useful for something. I may never have wanted to fight with anyone, but my older brother made sure I knew how to throw a decent jab," I said, rubbing my knuckles, remembering how sore they'd been for a few days.

"Smart brother," Jay said.

"About the rumors, though, I said them because I was mad, and it came out before I realized what I was saying. I hope you guys don't hate me for making it harder to find a date or whatever." I stopped myself, realizing that I was rambling because I was nervous.

"Why would we hate you for that?" Brayden asked.

I looked over at him as he stepped closer to me, then sat on his heels, so we were eye to eye. His beautiful hazel eyes shone with something I was scared to name, but looked a lot like desire.

"Well, I just became the biggest cockblock to the five of you. I can't imagine that was a helpful thing to do as a friend."

"Hmm, I can see that you might view it that way," Brayden said, bobbing his head and then turning his gaze to me, locking me in place. "What if we were all yours and not interested in anyone else?"

I laughed at his outlandish suggestion. "How could that ever be a real thing? I mean, for starters, I'm fairly positive that Micah doesn't like me as a person, let alone as a love interest."

"How the fuck did you come to that conclusion?" Micah barked, pulling my attention from Brayden.

"Um, case in point. I don't know if you've ever been nice to me since our unfortunate meeting at the library," I pointed out.

Micah stepped over to me and glowered down at me. "What do you call me taking a bath in soda to keep you from getting hit with it? Let's not even add the fact that I'm always watching your back when you're studying in the library alone at night. You saying that doesn't make us friends?"

I sat blinking at him, unable to answer, stunned by his words.

"Why do I even bother?" he said, throwing up his hands and stomping off.

Watching him walk away, I still had no idea what was going on. I leaned in closer to Brayden and whispered, "Am I dreaming right now?"

Brayden leaned in and kissed my cheek, letting it linger longer than normal. "I don't think so, unless we're having the same dream."

Brayden's eyes glowed with humor and heat, and he did not move back from my personal space. I slowly leaned back so I could think again, which I wasn't able to do when I was so close to him. Clearing my throat, I stood up, careful not to knock Brayden over.

"I need to use the ladies' room. I'll be right back," I said before I turned and bolted, needing some space from a situation I never thought I would be in.

Once in the bathroom, I splashed cold water on my face trying to calm the fuck down. I blotted my face gently with a paper towel, trying not to wash off all my makeup. I heard someone enter the bathroom, but didn't really bother to see who it was. Still bent over the sink, I didn't see the attack coming, but I felt it as my head was smashed into the porcelain sink. Then I blacked out.

I groaned as I sat up, my head pounding like I was kicked by a horse. I opened my eyes slowly and found that I wasn't in the bathroom but an open field in the middle of nowhere. Or that was my guess, since I couldn't see anything to give me a clue to where I was. The night sky was clear, and the moon was full, so the field was cast in a cold glow, making the whole scene look eerie.

"Little lamb, little lamb, I found you . . ."

The raspy voice grated on my nerves, sending me into a panic. *How could the creature from my nightmare be here? I dreamt that whole thing, there's no way it could be real.*

Out of the shadows, a person materialized a few feet in front of me. It was Mallory, but she was ashen, and her eyes were dead, unseeing orbs in her head. Her body was limp and seemed to move like a puppet on strings. I scrambled to my feet as the feeling of pure terror coursed through my body, and I froze at the vision before me. Black smoke seemed to pour out of her mouth, and when it was done, the body fell limply to the ground. The black smoke seemed to solidify into the shape of a creature that would only be in someone's nightmares.

It was tall and skeletal, the remaining flesh on it was black and charred, falling from him like ash. The face, if you could call it that, had no eyes, just a gaping mouth with rows of teeth. Even without eyes, it seemed to know right where I was, so it could see in some fashion. Its arms reached all the way down to its knees with long, sharply-pointed fingers. It reached out to me, its claws falling short by a mere inch.

"You won't get away from me this time, little lamb. I will have you and bring you to my master. He will be most pleased with me." It stepped forward in a strange, disjointed way, like it didn't really know how to use its legs.

"Why does your master want me?" I stammered, trying desperately to understand what was going on.

It cocked its head at me as if it didn't understand the question. "The little lamb doesn't know?" It laughed, the sound as grating as rocks crashing to the ground. "The angels' weapon is clueless to its power. I am truly lucky to have been given this task."

"You're right, I have no idea what the hell you're talking about. You must have me mistaken for someone else," I said, clinging to that hope.

"No, little lamb, you may not know what you are, but I do." It raised its hand again and let a claw-like finger scrape down my cheek hard enough that I felt it begin to bleed. "Your power is close, but you have not owned it yet. Pity we will never see what you will become. I imagine the heaven's light would have shone brightly from you, little lamb, or should I say, little Synergy."

If I hadn't already been frozen where I stood, that one word would have done it. Synergy, the sixth element, according to Aydin Ryevick, that was to be the most powerful element of them all. Why would this creature be bringing that up now?

"I have delayed enough, now I must end you and bring your lifeless body to my master," the creature said, pulling his hand back and straightening two fingers, readying to slit my throat.

My terror bubbled up in my throat strangling any cry for help. I railed against my fear and the power that was holding me frozen in place. I cried out with everything I had, desperate to live and save myself. Hot tears streamed down my face, stinging in the cut on my cheek. Finally, my voice returned, and I screamed loud and long, hoping anyone would be able to hear me and come to my rescue. With that cry, I felt something deep inside me crack and burst, filling my body with explosive power.

My back bowed at the force of my power. It shot out of my hands and my mouth, seeking escape where it could, trying to free my body from its dark hold. With that surge of power, my body was freed, and I fell to my knees, gasping for breath. My throat burned as if I had just swallowed an ember. I blinked a few times, trying to clear my eyes from the golden haze that clouded them.

"It seems that the little Elementi had found her spark," the creature said, its voice no longer as sure as it once was. It had taken a step back from me and shrank away from the golden light I was surrounded by.

My power-filled body flowed with the knowledge that this was a demon, and he was the enemy. I had no idea where the knowledge came from, but I didn't argue with it. Unfortunately, I didn't know what to do about it. Before I could come up with any sort of plan or idea, the demon attacked, lashing out at me with its talons. Still on my knees, I rolled out of the way and surged to my feet, keeping the demon in my eyesight. I sorted through the things I learned at the self-defense classes, but nothing was going to help me in this scenario. It wasn't trying to hold me and take me somewhere, no, this attacker was trying to kill me.

"Lailah, duck!" Hudson's voice called out of the darkness.

Without hesitating, I dropped to the ground. Gunshots went off, and the demon staggered back with two glowing blue bullet holes in its chest. It was followed up by an arrow to the middle of its head, knocking it to the ground. Parker charged up to the demon with a glowing purple staff that had a blade attached to the end of it. The demon was trying to stand, but in one fluid move, Parker severed its head. The force of the hit sent the head flying off into the field and out of sight. Micah strode forward, glowing from some internal light that made it seem like he was an ember in the dark of night. Fire shot out of his hands, engulfing the demon's body in flames until it was reduced to ashes.

Slowly, I made it up on my knees, but I knew I wasn't ready to try and stand. Jay, holding a glowing white bow, walked over to me and crouched, looking me over. "Are you okay?"

I tried to nod my head yes but the power that had receded with their arrival burst forth again, drowning me until all I could see was golden light. I was drifting, lost in the swirling golden light of a power that I knew was held in my body. It had been dormant, waiting for the right time to be released. No, that wasn't right. It was waiting for the right people, who I was meant to find, to show up, and now they were here with me.

"Lailah Mackenzie, chosen bearer of the element Synergy, you have been awakened at last," a soft lilting voice said.

Slowly, my eyes cleared only to be blinded by a bright white light as if I was staring into the sun. I raised a hand to shield my face from the rays. I could make out an outline of a figure dressed in white with large wings flared out on either side.

"Am I dead?"

"No, sweet child, you are very much alive for the first time. The promise has been fulfilled in you, Lailah. We angels chose you to be the light in a dark world. With your help, the Elementi will be able to free the world of the Dark Master's influence."

"Why me?" I asked, dumbfounded.

"You are exactly what each of those boys needs in their lives and the same for you. This group of men was never meant to be a group of five, they always needed a sixth to balance them out. With you beside them, great work can be done, the like of which no other blessed Elementi Warriors have done before."

"I don't understand any of this, what is happening to me?" I said, feeling like I was going to lose my mind with all the questions I had.

"Trust in them, child, we picked them just as we have picked you. These men will guide you through this. I must send you back now, I have kept you too long, and they grow fearful for you." The angel reached out and touched my cheek, the same one the demon had scratched. "The wards must be renewed in order to keep you all safe. I will give you this knowledge so that you may rest easy while you learn. It will not hold them off for long, though, they grow in strength and numbers."

The angel bent down and placed a kiss on my forehead, sending a spark of energy through me. "Blessing upon you, child, we will see each other again." With those parting words, the angel thrust me back into my body back in the fields.

"Lailah. Lailah!" someone yelled, shaking me and making me grunt at the abuse.

"Stop, Micah, you're hurting her," Brayden said, and the shaking stopped.

I pried an eye open, unsure if I really wanted to wake up just yet. I saw the guys' worried faces hovering around me. I decided that I was just going to have to suck it up and deal with what was happening around me. I let Micah help me into a sitting position, and then I reached out to Hudson, who pulled me to my feet.

"Fuck, I never want to do that again, it hurts way too much," I whined, rubbing my temples.

"Yeah, it's been years since I came into my powers, but I remember what a bitch it was," Parker said with a grimace.

"We should get you back to the house; the first time your powers show up takes a lot out of you," Brayden said, resting his hands on my shoulders.

I leaned back into him, welcoming the support. "Unfortunately for me, it's not quite over yet."

"What do you mean?" Jay asked.

"We have to fix the wards before the night is over," I stated.

"How the fuck do you know about that?" Micah demanded.

I smirked at him and the shock on his face. "Had a lovely chat with an angel a moment ago."

"You're handling this all surprisingly well. Too well for my liking," Hudson said, eyeing me.

"A combination of exhaustion and denial is a potent cocktail for dealing with mental breakdowns. Give me a little bit, and I'm sure I'll be a hysterical puddle on the ground in no time." I took a deep breath and held out my hands. "Now, let's get this over with while I'm still in a delusional state."

Brayden took my left hand, Hudson my right, and the others followed suit, so we were one large circle. Closing my eyes, I let the information the angel gave me come to the forefront of my thoughts.

"We, the Elementi, ask for blessing on this sacred ground. With fire we burn back the darkness, with spirit we guard the souls of those we protect, with earth we replenish the purity of our lands, and with water and air we cleanse the evils from areas we hold dominion over." As I spoke, I could feel the flare of power from the corresponding barrier of the element. "Binding together the powers of the blessed Warriors, I, Synergy, light of the heavens, anoint this land."

As the words left my mouth, I felt each of the guys' power shoot into me like arrows into a target. I held tight to their hands as I fell to my knees under the weight of their energy residing in me. I swirled it into a little ball, wrapped neatly in my own power, and thrust it into the ground at my feet. The earth rumbled with our combined power, and the wards began to glow in my mind's eye, replenished and stronger than they'd ever been. Done with the task that I was given by the angel, my power drained from me, as did the last bit of strength to hold myself up. I was lowered to the ground by the guys, and I sat there relearning how to breathe.

Holy shit! I was Synergy, and the five guys I'd been hanging around were the Elementi. I knew they were real! But that was going to have to wait for another day, I was too tired to even try to process everything. I felt my body being lifted, and I was carried away somewhere, but I wasn't worried. I was with my guys, and they would look after me and protect me. As the angel said, they were meant for me, but what they didn't know yet was I was made for them and only them.

Twenty-Three

Brayden

I held onto Lailah's arm as she crumpled to the ground after she renewed the wards. I could feel her power draining from her, taking the last of her strength with it. Bending down, I went to scoop her up, but Micah gathered her in his arms before I could. Raising an eyebrow, I looked at him.

"You have clean-up duty. I've got her," Micah said as he cradled her against his chest.

He'd been the only one of us fighting against what having Synergy here now meant, but it seemed that Lailah might have found a way to get under that thick skin of his. I knew Micah was afraid to let himself care, but Lailah was hard to resist.

"We need to get her back to the house; we can't let her stay in the dorms until we know she can manage her power," Micah said, walking off toward the car.

Parker stepped up next to me, watching Micah's back and shaking his head. "Do you think he's possessed?"

"Why would you ask that?" I asked, frowning at Parker.

"Um, because Micah just had his power manipulated by Synergy. The one true villain who is going to wreck our lives, and now, he's clutching her to his chest like she might disappear on him."

I sighed at his words. He wasn't wrong. "Yeah, but none of us was prepared for it to be Lailah. Who would have guessed the most powerful blessed Elementi Warrior would appear in the body of a girl who gets lost in her own room. Lord, she finds more trouble than any human could manage, and acts like it's nothing."

"Until it comes to us. She lost her shit on that one," Parker said, grinning.

"Speaking of that. How do you think we should tell her what being Synergy entails?" Hudson asked, joining in our conversation.

"Fuck, not me, I don't need her mad at me now that I know what that looks like," Parker said, shivering dramatically.

That reminded me about Mallory, and I found Jay crouching next to her, examining the body. We all knew that she was dead the moment the demon used her as a host to get past the weakened wards. It was sad to say that it was no great loss for us that she was gone. I was sad that an innocent bystander in our fight had to lose her life though, even if she'd been a bitter, selfish person.

"Find anything useful?" I called out to Jay.

He shook his head and stepped back from the body. "Nope, clean kill, no markings or demon trace on her. You can do your thing, we won't learn anything more from her."

I wasn't proud of the fact that I'd buried many such bodies deep in the earth, but we couldn't leave behind any evidence of the demon's attack. Closing my eyes, I pulled the earth apart under her body and let it fall where no one would find her. Letting the ground close back up without any sign that anything had happened, we all headed after Micah.

My phone started to vibrate in my back pocket, and I pulled it out to see it was Beth calling.

"Hey Beth, we got to her in time. We're all headed back to the house," I said, knowing what she was going to ask.

"Thank God, how did we let her get taken from under our noses?" Beth asked, sounding tired.

"The demon possessed another student's body and must've used it to get close to Lailah. With it hiding in human skin, the wards wouldn't have been activated in their weakened state. Once it was out of the host, we got to her as soon as we could."

"Did her powers present?"

"You could say that. We just did the ritual to renew the wards. From what I can feel, they are stronger than ever. Beth, I've never seen anything like it, she took a thread of each of our powers and bound them together to do it."

"Are you telling me the ground shaking was her?"

"Yeah, that's what I'm telling you. Try standing next to her while she's doing it. That shit's fucking intense."

"Brayden, language," Beth chided. "I didn't raise you boys to have such foul mouths."

She never seemed to scold the others when they swore. Just me. Maybe it's because I didn't do it very often.

"We'll be at the house soon. Do you have a room set up for her?"

Beth huffed at me. "Of course I do! There's been a room ready for her before she even landed in the country."

"I should've known better than to question you," I said before I hung up and hopped into Jay's jeep. We took off with Parker following us on his bike.

Once back at the house, we all filed in behind Micah, who was still holding Lailah. Beth met us at the entrance. "Micah, her room is going to be the north one off the common room."

Beth opened the door for him, flipping on the light so he could make his way to the bed without running into something. As he settled her, Beth drew back the blackout curtains, so the moonlight shone in through the glass French doors.

"I want to make sure if she wakes up in the night, she can see her surroundings," Beth said, answering our questioning looks. "We should also have someone stay here, so when she does come around, she won't be freaked out by being in an unfamiliar place."

"I'll stay," I said before any of the others could volunteer. "If she starts freaking out when she wakes up, I have the ability to ground her powers. I've done it once before."

Beth nodded her head. "Sounds like a good plan, but I want to chat with you all a moment. Let's step out into the living room, so we don't wake her."

Stepping out of her room brought us to the hub of the house. It was a common area that we called the living room that each of our bedrooms faced. If we weren't in the library, chances were, we were here. I settled into my favorite battered leather armchair, and the others ended up in their respective spots around the room.

"Things are going to change for Lailah now that her power has manifested. I'm going to need your help making this transition as smooth as possible. If she is as powerful as you say, Brayden, I don't want her tearing down the house around our ears," Beth said, perched on the edge of the couch cushion.

"She's going to have tons of questions when she wakes up; how do you want me to handle that?" I asked.

"Manage what you can, but I would like to have a face-to-face chat with her. I realize that she's comfortable with all of you, but I need to start building my rapport with her since I'm going to be the one she comes to with her needs." Beth sighed, rubbing her temple. "Once she finds out that I knew all along, I have a feeling she's going to be very angry with me. I can't say I blame her, but I hope she will see the reason."

"Have Cami here for that conversation. That will help," Parker pointed out.

"If you're straight with her and give her facts, she will handle it much better than appealing to her emotions," Hudson offered.

"Letting her know that no other secrets will be held from her is also going to be something she needs to hear. Her having access to everything and everywhere will prove that to her," Micah said, surprising me that he realized that about her.

"Getting her back into a routine as fast as possible will give her some stability," Jay added, drawing everyone's attention.

Beth smiled at us like a proud mom. "My, it seems you've really figured her out."

"It's not that hard. She's an open book to those she feels comfortable around," I said, shrugging my shoulders.

"That brings me to the other thing I wanted to address." Beth's demeanor changed, and she shifted from the loving mom into the fierce protector, pinning us all with a pointed stare. "I expect all of you to treat her with the respect she deserves. We always knew that you would need to bond with Synergy, and now seeing it's a woman, it's not lost on me how that will happen. Not the way you have been attracted to her like moths to a flame. Hear me on this, boys. If any of you disrespects that sacred bond and the gift that it is, heaven help protect you from my wrath. Do I make myself clear?"

We all bobbed our heads in agreement, each of us having experienced Beth's anger at least once in our lives. It was something none of us wanted to repeat.

"Excellent! I'm going to fill Cami in on what's been happening while she was enjoying the party and failing to do her job," Beth said, smiling at us once again.

I did not envy Cami and the hell she was going to pay when Beth was done with her.

"Don't ream her out too badly; we told her that we would take care of Lailah while she had a little fun. We're as much at fault as anyone," Parker said, speaking up for Cami.

"Oh, I'm fully aware you *all* fucked up tonight, Parker. It would be wise for you not to remind me of it while I'm feeling forgiving," Beth said as she left the living room.

"Shit, did you hear her drop the f-bomb?" Hudson said, cradling his head in his hands. "We are so fucked; I don't even want to find out what our punishment will be."

"Nothing we can do about it now. Might as well make the best of it," I said, standing and heading to my room.

I wanted to change before I camped out in Lailah's room for the night. Once out of my Halloween costume and in comfy sweatpants, I quietly entered Lailah's room, which was lit only by the light of the full moon. Looking at her lying on the bed in her yellow dress made her look like some fairy tale princess. I walked over to her, brushed a few rogue curls out of her face, and let my fingers trail down her cheek. She moved into my touch as if even in her sleep, she knew it was me. Sitting down next to her, I studied her face. I looked at her for the first time as Synergy, the sixth element. Her skin seemed to glow with a faint golden light, her power pulsing just under her skin. I reached out, took her hand in mine, pulled it up to my lips, and kissed the back of it. I let my lips linger longer than I should have, but it was harder to fight her pull now that her power was released.

I set her hand back down and tried to move away, but she clutched my wrist as if her life depended on it. Unable to keep myself from grinning, I let myself be trapped by her. As the minutes passed, I realized she wasn't going to let go of me, so I did the only thing I could. I stretched out beside her, letting the length of my body rest against hers. Letting out a contented sigh, I watched as she nuzzled into me as though having me here was a normal occurrence. If the others were to find out about this, they would be so pissed, but that was a risk I was gladly willing to take. They were going to need to learn to share her sooner or later because she was ours to treasure and protect for the rest of our lives.

To be continued in Refining Earth

About Author

Elizabeth is an International Best Seller, originally from Illinois but now living in sunny Phoenix, AZ. Elizabeth has been writing for nine years and started out in YA Fiction but recently found herself loving the Reverse Harem genre. Like her favorite books, Elizabeth loves to write about strong women of all varieties. Not all strength is flashy or apparent at first glance—some lies just under the surface.

Don't Miss Out!

Be the first to know what is coming next by following Elizabeth's social media! You never know when or what will be coming next!

Website: ElizabethKnightBooks.com

Facebook: Elizabeth Knight's Unicorn Queens

Instagram: elizabethknightauthor

TikTok: elizabethknightauthor

Newsletter: sign up here

Also By

<u>Standalone Books</u>

Lying Lainey: Underground Omega Syndicate (May 2023)

Nicolette: Ladies of the MC (April 2023)

<u>Hidden Empire Series – Complete series</u>

Book 1 - Two Tricks

Book 2 - Three Tricks

Book 3 - Four Tricks

Book 4 - More Tricks

Book 5 - Our Tricks

<u>Hidden Empire Novel</u>

Harper's Renegades

<u>Omega Assassin - Complete series</u>

Book 1 - Dual Nature

Book 2 - Hidden Nature

Book 3 - Perfect Nature

www.ingramcontent.com/pod-product-compliance
Lightning Source LLC
Chambersburg PA
CBHW070505300726